Murder In A Small Town

By Don Lawrence

Copyright 2017
Don Lawrence

Murder In A Small Town

Contents

Chapter One: Two Pools 4

Chapter Two: The All-American Couple 11

Chapter Three: A Fountain And A Fatality 24

Chapter Four: The Back Porch 35

Chapter Five: Looking For Evidence 46

Chapter Six: Two Friends 61

Chapter Seven: Messenger of Death 70

Chapter Eight: Work The Case 92

Chapter Nine: Questions 128

Chapter Ten: Guilty, But Innocent? 154

Chapter Eleven: Suspects 172

Chapter Twelve: Best Friends 196

Chapter Thirteen: Innocent, But Guilty? 210

Chapter Fourteen: Home Sweet Home 229

Chapter Fifteen: A Warrant 264

Chapter Sixteen: With Friends Like This... 299

Chapter Seventeen: Murder In A Small Town 322

Chapter 18: Epilogue 332

Murder In A Small Town

Chapter One: Two Pools

The weapon pierced her blouse, tore open her chest and penetrated into the chest cavity, creating a wound which was fatal. Her life's blood was rushing out of her, forming a sticky mess which a friend would soon find, but by then, it would be too late. When she awoke that morning, the thought had never crossed her mind that she would be dead within a few hours. She had no idea whatsoever that her life was in danger. There was no reason for her to even think of such a thing. But then, how many who are murdered anticipate their demise? One minute she was at peace, contented, smiling, happy ... the next minute, she was dead.

There are many things which can drastically change a small town. The closing of a mill. The building of an interstate highway. The devastation of a tornado. In Springerville, it was a murder. From that day on, the murder became the mark of time, as in, "I moved here two years before the murder" or "I graduated from high school a year after the murder" or "Our youngest son was actually born the same week as the murder." This was not only the news of the day, nor the news of the year, in small town Springerville, it was the tragic event which scarred the history of this otherwise quiet and peaceful community.

    The autumn day had begun as most days in small towns often do. The paper boy, Dennis Fisher, after folding all of the newspapers and fitting them into the carry bags, delivered his papers, throwing them from his bike as he rode through the neighborhoods. Occasionally hitting the porch, but more often landing in the general direction of it. Men and women made their way into the mill, carrying their lunch buckets and discussing the chance of rain for that weekend. Elderly couples sat on their front porch, enjoying the peaceful, cool autumn morning while looking at the leaves on the trees which had begun to turn to their various shades of yellow, orange and red. The high school marching band, having arrived on campus early for their daily practice, tried to match musical rhythm with marching cadence as they worked through their numbers, preparing for Friday night's home football game.

    The school bus made its rounds, picking up children who were still trying to rub the sleep from their eyes. Dale Edwards had been driving the Springerville school bus for as long as the townsfolk could remember. As the bus turned onto Main Street, the children crowded to the right side of the bus to get a better view of what appeared to be a mini-geyser, spraying majestically in front of Truman's Market.

    Dale looked into the mirror to see all the kids crammed to one side of the bus as they tried to maximize their view and said to the children, "You kids get back in your seats. You can't be running around like a bunch of wild Indians while you're on a bus!" The kids slowly made their way back to their seats while simultaneously trying to get a look at what had happened.

    One of the older boys, Jonathan, said, "Mr. Edwards, you aren't supposed to say Indians. You're supposed to say Native Americans."

"Thank you Jonathan," Dale replied shaking his head and smiling, "you are correct," realizing again that he was a plain spoken man in a politically correct world.

The fire hydrant, which had capped the water line now spraying without restriction into the air, lay demolished on the ground next to the source of the fountain. While trying to parallel park, old lady Perkins had accidentally backed her 1964 Buick up over the curb and into the hydrant. After hearing the crushing sound of her bumper striking, well, something, she slowly pulled her vehicle off the curb and back into the street. Her car was now sitting at an awkward angle to the curb. She could neither identify the sudden whooshing sound nor understand the sudden deluge of water falling upon her car.

Her family had tried to persuade Anne Perkins on several occasions that it was time for her to stop driving. They feared that she would someday be injured in an accident, or injure someone else. But old lady Perkins liked her independence and resolutely refused to give up her drivers license or her cherished vehicle. She still wasn't sure exactly what had happened, yet intuitively she somehow knew she was the cause of something that could only be trouble. She knew immediately that this was a game changer. Her heart sunk, not just because of this little accident, but because she knew this would be the end of her driving. A tear ran down her cheek as she watched the water from the now broken fire line begin to puddle in the street.

Meanwhile, laying in a puddle of blood on a back porch not more than five miles from the sudden Main Street fountain, lay the body of Stacy Pruitt. Murdered earlier that morning, not yet missing, body still undiscovered. Normally the Main Street Fountain, as it was quickly dubbed, would be the talk of the town and ultimately work its way into the "remember when" stories told at high school reunions, social gatherings and family get-togethers. But, in fact, it became nothing more than an afterthought, a footnote to the biggest story to ever rock the world of Springerville. Stacy Pruitt had been murdered. While water spewed high into the air along Main Street, while children pointed and laughed at the gushing fountain, while several individuals tried to calm down old lady Perkins - Stacy lay in a pool of her own blood, undiscovered. As of yet, nobody knew. They did not know she was dead. They did not know who killed her. They did not know why she was killed. But that would soon change.

Chapter Two: The All-American Couple

Stacy Pruitt was one of the many residents who had grown up in Springerville. It was a close-knit community. Many had been born here, many more had moved here while they were young children. The mill was the main source of employment, but there were other small businesses and a few small farms in the area. It seemed that everybody knew everyone in Springerville. Some, perhaps, knew more than they should, or so others thought. Having neighbors who were relatives or extended relatives was not uncommon. Likewise, having relatives at your place of employment was not rare. One might correctly surmise that it was a typical small town in middle America.

Stacy was born right here in Springerville at the local medical center. The medical center wasn't large enough to be considered a hospital, but it served the community well. That service included the delivery over the years of many of the current residents, Stacy included. She, like most of the others, was delivered by old Dr. Clevenger. He was an old school general practitioner dealing with everything from runny noses, to broken bones, to stitching up cuts on fingers and arms, to delivering babies. He had seen Stacy, and many others, grow from infancy to young adulthood. Now retired, he was somewhat of an icon and still highly respected in the community.

While growing up, Stacy did what most little girls did in Springerville. When not in school, she took dancing classes: tap, ballet, and contemporary. She had sleepovers with her girlfriends and picnics with her family. She was in Girl Scouts and was active in her church Sunday School classes, Vacation Bible School and, as she got older, church youth camps. Like many young girls, she kept a diary. Of course, no one was allowed to read that diary, except her very best friend, Dotty Miller. The two shared their deepest secrets and often would giggle and laugh as they talked about different boys at school. Stacy was popular as a child and that popularity carried on into her teen years.

When she got into high school, she tried out for the cheerleading squad and was an easy pick to make the cheer team. Her dancing skills, as well as her natural beauty, including her flowing blond hair, emerald green eyes and a slight dusting of freckles across her nose and cheeks, no doubt worked to her advantage in being selected. By her senior year, she was captain of the cheerleaders. Her studies came easy to her and thus she did well in school in regards to her grades. Not that academics were important to her. Homework and other assignments were quickly dealt with so that she could get on with things she enjoyed, mostly socializing.

Nobody was surprised when she became homecoming queen her senior year, nor when she dated Shane Pruitt, the football quarterback, baseball pitcher, forward on the basketball team and, not coincidentally, homecoming king. She was the epitome of the all-American girl and they, the all-American couple. Their marriage just a few years after high school left no one surprised and seemed to please most. But, not everyone.

Shane Pruitt was not born in Springerville; he had moved there when he was six years old. He grew up the youngest of three boys. All three boys grew up participating in sports. Little league baseball, soccer, peewee football, basketball ... sports kept the boys busy and for the most part, out of trouble. They had each started Boy Scouts, but each had eventually come to the same conclusion; it just wasn't for them. Sports was their world, and they excelled in that arena - especially Shane. Playing with, and competing against, his older brothers ultimately made him a better athlete when competing against boys his own age and size. The shelves in his bedroom were all loaded with trophies, ribbons and plaques, all won in league after league, year after year. He was first and foremost a jock. By his junior year in high school he stood six feet one inch tall, making him the tallest of the three Pruitt boys. Although his two older brothers would never admit it, he was also the best athlete of the three. This, coupled with his quick smile, handsome looks and wavy jet black hair, gave him a confidence which served him well athletically as well as socially.

As such, he was one of the popular kids on campus. He was used to the special attention he received, and he liked that attention. His school grades were good, but not great. They were perhaps better than he deserved. Teachers, either consciously or sub-consciously, tended to go just a little bit easier on the school's star athlete. So did the principal. So, when Shane was caught drinking beer in the parking lot one afternoon after school, the principal gave him a stern lecture, but no suspension, as most other students would have received. When Shane and some of his friends taunted, teased and eventually locked one of the smaller boys in a locker after gym class, his football coach, Coach Stewart, joked about it with his guys in private and simply suggested that they probably shouldn't do that again. When the small boy's parents complained to the coach about the bullying their son had received, Coach tried to convince the parents that it was just the other boys' way of making their son feel part of their group. The parents weren't naive enough to believe him, but didn't know where else to turn. So, for Shane and his friends, drinking and picking on smaller kids was not a rare activity.

Shane and Stacy grew up knowing each other, but hung out with different groups of friends until their junior year in high school. Both were attractive, both were popular, one excelled at sports, the other excelled at cheering for those in sports. It was only a matter of time before their paths crossed, they became friends, and started dating. They soon were going steady and dating each other exclusively, although Shane would occasionally forget the concept of exclusivity, a problem which haunted their relationship even into their short years of marriage.

After high school, Shane received a football scholarship to the state university located in a larger town approximately 130 miles from Springerville. He quickly came to realize that he was no longer the big fish in the little pond. Others on the college football team were at least as big and fast as Shane, most were in fact bigger and faster. He was good, but he was now competing against boys who were as good or better. His first year he practiced with the team, but was not officially on the team. Frustrated, he contemplated quitting and going to a smaller college. But his father encouraged, or rather, insisted that he stay and see if he would fare better the following year. He was still growing, working out, training, improving ... he had a good chance if he stayed focused.

But therein lay the problem. Living away from home for the first time proved to be a challenge, as it did for many young adults in his situation. At the university, there were no shortage of social gatherings, parties, clowning around with the guys, and other distractions which would keep him from his studies and his workouts. And girls; he had never seen so many beautiful girls in one location, many of whom enjoyed the same social scene and parties that Shane frequented. He was still committed to Stacy, but she was attending a smaller school in another town. And while the cat's away ...

By his junior year in college, Shane had indeed worked his way onto the football team. He had made it! But he wasn't a starter. In fact, he was third string quarterback. The first and second string quarterbacks were seniors, so Shane figured that if he paid his dues this year, he'd have a real good shot at being the starter next year. During the week he ran plays on the scout team against the first team defense. Because he was with other third stringers, he took a beating on a regular basis. This ultimately led to the end of his football career.

Midway through that third season, at midweek practice while playing quarterback on the scout team, Shane dropped back to pass. As he set his feet and began to throw, an undersized third string guard was blocked back into him by a blitzing linebacker. Both boys came crashing into the outside of Shane's knee, tearing both inside and outside ligaments and damaging the kneecap. Shane had played his last down as a football player. His lifelong dream of being a professional quarterback came crashing down upon him. His short-lived football career was over.

Shane wanted to quit school and head back home. His father, as one might expect, insisted that Shane stay in school and focus on his studies. His father argued that Shane had been given a scholarship and should not let such an opportunity for a good education slip away. After reconstructive surgery for his knee, he took the rest of the semester off to recuperate. While at home, his father continued to encourage him to return to college and finish his degree. They ultimately reached a compromise; Shane would transfer to the same college in which Stacy was enrolled and he would finish his degree there.

The spring semester found Shane and Stacy sharing an apartment while finishing the last year and a half of their degree. However, Stacy never finished. One month before the end of the semester of her junior year, Stacy announced that she was pregnant. She was elated; Shane was concerned. She always wanted to be a stay at home mom, married to a wonderful man, raising their children and growing old together in her beloved Springerville. In her mind, Shane would always be her big man on campus: popular, handsome, fun, dashing, her Mr. Wonderful.

Shane wasn't certain he was ready to be married and certainly didn't think he was ready to be a dad. He seemed to still be recovering emotionally from the destruction of his dreams of football stardom. He was just getting back into the groove of college life. This time, though, he did a little more studying and a little less partying.

But he did love Stacy and she had been there for him during his rehabilitation of his knee. He had certainly enjoyed living with her during their few months back together. So, he accepted his fate, proposed marriage, tried to get his mind around being a dad and set his sights on finishing his schooling. Before the school year was over, Stacy Young had become Mrs. Stacy Pruitt. Shane's brother, Trent, was the best man at their wedding, while Stacy's longtime friend, Dotty Miller was the maid of honor.

Shane did indeed finish his last year of college, earning a degree in Physical Education with a minor in Mathematical Studies. While he excelled in the former, he barely got by in the latter, and that only with Stacy's help. Nonetheless, he had his degree and it did lead to a few teaching/coaching offers from around the state. But he had his heart set on one job. He wanted to go home. Home to where he had been a hero, where he was successful, where his family and many of his friends still lived. So, he applied and was hired at Springerville High School. He would teach a couple of beginning math classes and a few P.E. classes. He would also immediately become the offensive coordinator and assistant to the head coach for the varsity football team, Coach Stewart, the same coach he had played for during his high school years. The hometown hero had come home and had received a hero's welcome when he did.

Upon returning to Springerville, Shane and Stacy quickly settled into married life and raising a family. Their first child, Kortnee, was a cute little blond haired daughter with a striking resemblance to her mother. At the baby shower, she received more tiny cheerleader outfits than any other gift. The all-American couple now had an all-American child.

But appearances can be misleading. No one knew that this perfect couple had an imperfect marriage. No one would have guessed that divorce was in their future. No one would have imagined that one day, Stacy would be murdered.

Chapter Three: A Fountain And A Fatality

Chief of Police, Frederick Earl, had instructed one of his officers, Aaron Renner, to direct traffic on Main Street. The fountain had attracted a crowd which added to the morning rush hour, if it can actually be called that in a small town. Dale Edwards had gotten all the children back into their seats and the school bus had gone on its way, taking the kids to school. The children on the bus felt that they were the lucky ones. They'd be the ones telling all the other kids about the fountain of water and old lady Perkins and her car.

The fire department had arrived quickly, but Fire Chief Gary Patrick had to wait for the water department to shut off the main water line.

"Morning Gary," Chief Earl said to the fire chief.

"Morning Fred," Chief Patrick responded.

Most in the town referred to them by title and last name. But these two heads of their departments had known each other and worked together for years. They had become close friends during that time. The formality of titles and last names had given way a long time ago, with the exception of filling out official reports or speaking of the other in an official capacity or public meeting. But this was not one of those situations.

"Don't happen to have a spare hydrant in the back of your truck, do you," the police chief asked, smiling.

Chief Patrick chuckled and said, "Nope. That's not standard equipment on one of these rigs. But we do have one at the station. In fact, why don't you run on over and pick that up for me?"

The chief laughed and retorted, "Well, we certainly wouldn't want to overwork you this morning. No doubt this interrupted some soap opera you were watching at the station?"

"Not at all. In fact, we were out on a traffic accident call early this morning out on the highway. But that was probably before you got out of bed," the fire chief responded, "I just figured that you could swing by the station and pick up the hydrant on your way to getting your morning supply of donuts."

"Oh, that's original," the chief said, smiling and shaking his head.

"Sorry, Fred," the fire chief said, "That was just too easy." He then added, "I've already sent one of our crew, Kevin Darren, over to pick up the hydrant."

"Great!" said Chief Earl. "Now if we can just get the water company over here, we can get this mess cleaned up."

Chief Frederick Earl had joined the Army shortly after graduating from high school. The last year of his four year service, he became an M.P. on his base. He had not planned on being a part of the Military Police, but several of his buddies were and his commanding officer encouraged him to do so. Much to his surprise, he enjoyed police work. He didn't try to be a tough guy, as happened to some when they put on the police uniform. But neither did he put up with any nonsense from those with whom he dealt. He believed that in most cases, if you treated others fairly and with respect, they would do the same to you. In those moments when he really needed to be tough, he was more than up to the task.

When he was discharged from the military, he enrolled in college and took several criminal justice classes. Eventually, he attended the police academy and, upon graduation, secured a job in Chicago. He worked hard, kept out of trouble, and rose through the ranks. After twelve years, he decided that big city life and big city police work was not to his liking. He began looking for a job in a small town with a small department. This led to his employment in Springerville.

When Fred hired on at Springerville, he was hired as assistant to the chief, who, at that time was Rick Forrest. The chief was three years away from retirement and the agreement was that Chief Forrest would endorse Fred in regards to being his successor for the position of Chief of Police at the end of that third year. Chief Forrest was a happy-go-lucky, gregarious individual, well liked by the decision makers in the community, which included the Town Manager, the Mayor, and the Town Council. Thus, with the chief's endorsement, three years after moving to town, Frederick Earl became the Chief of the Springerville Police Department.

The residents who did not already know him quickly learned that he was not at all like his predecessor. Chief Earl was not a back-slapping, joke telling, life of the party, man-about-town. His focus was simply doing his job to the best of his ability. He quickly became known as a no-nonsense kind of guy. His six foot two inch, two hundred thirty pounds, lent itself to that reputation. The old scar on his forehead above his left eye added to his tough guy reputation. The scar was the result of a bar room brawl that he and another M.P. had to break up back in his army days. The individual who had blind sided him with a cue stick across Fred's forehead soon regretted that cheap shot. With blood pouring down his face, Fred literally threw the guy through the front window of the bar, and the brawl abruptly ended. While the drunken soldier received several stitches, Fred received a nasty scar and a reprimand for his efforts. Except for a very few select friends, most never knew how he got the scar. When asked, he would simply reply, "That was a long time ago and we don't talk about that anymore." Thus, scar rumors were rampant. Everything from an old war injury to taking down a drug lord in Chicago were included in those rumors. He paid them no mind.

First and foremost, Fred was fair. He was always polite and respectful. He demanded the same from his staff. In every aspect of the job, he demanded a high standard of conduct for himself as well as from his officers. As such, he quickly gained the respect of the vast majority of the citizens of Springerville.

He enjoyed life in Springerville. He and his wife, Diane, did not have any children. They had several close friends and very much enjoyed activities with those friends. These were the ones who saw a side of Fred that most never did. His sense of humor, his teasing, his love of outdoors, his appreciation of a nice glass of Merlot, a barbeque in the backyard with one or two other couples. No big parties. Nothing extravagant. His favorite moments were cruising around a mountain lake on his small pontoon boat, trolling for trout.

Twenty minutes after Chief Earl and Fire Chief Patrick had finished their discussion while standing on Main Street, the water company arrived and shut off the flow of water. Once the source of the water had been stopped, the repair work to the fire hydrant began immediately. Water had to be shut off for the surrounding area of Main Street, which included merchants and nearby residents. All were anxious to know how soon water service would be restored. Fortunately, the spare hydrant at the station was not more than two blocks away. It was retrieved and installed and water service restored not more than ninety minutes after Anne Perkins had decapitated the old hydrant.

Anne's old Buick was drivable, although the rear bumper and tail lights would need to be replaced and a slight amount of body work would need to be done to the rear of the car. Her family offered to pay for the hydrant and Mrs. Perkins was issued a citation. This would indeed end her days of driving.

As the mess was finally being cleaned up, Chief Earl received a call on his radio from his secretary, Michelle London, who also served as the local dispatch. The call was to inform him that Stacy Pruitt had been found in a pool of blood, dead. The Chief, hardly believing what he had just heard, asked Michelle to repeat the message. He had heard correctly - Stacy Pruitt was dead. He asked where her body was found and was told that she was on the porch of her home. After getting the address, he told Officer Aaron to follow him, then immediately headed to the home.

He arrived at the home and found Josh Allen sitting on the front porch. Josh was a multi-talented handyman who did a variety of odd jobs around town. His excellent craftsmanship and kind and gentle spirit kept him extremely busy in his trade. So much so that he had hired his childhood friend, Steve Winter, to be his assistant. Josh arrived that morning intent on doing some reconstructive repair work on the back porch before painting the porch. It was then that he found the body of Stacy laying on the porch. He immediately called the police station.

Josh was one of the many residents who had been born and raised in Springerville. He had married his high school sweetheart, Andrea Nicholas. Andrea and Stacy had been friends growing up. They had taken dance classes together and had both been in Girl Scouts. In high school they drifted apart, hanging out with different groups of friends and pursuing different interests. Andrea graduated from the Art Institute and became a graphic designer while Josh earned his degree at a trade school where he honed his many natural skills. Their two children, Caleb and Jacob, now kept them very busy. They enjoyed living in the town in which they had grown up, being near their parents and their many friends.

Josh, having known Stacy since they were children, knew immediately who it was when he found her on the back porch. When he called the police station, Michelle hardly recognized his trembling voice, even though she, too, had known him since childhood. She gasped when Josh told her the news. She wondered, but only for a split second, if this was another of Josh's pranks. He had been known to prank her before, but she reasoned that not even Josh would joke about such a thing. She then immediately got on the radio to give the chief the tragic news.

Chapter Four: The Back Porch

Aaron Rennner had worked for Chief Earl for sixteen years. As such, he was the senior officer on staff and, many assumed, the heir apparent to the chief when it came time for him to retire. But, that was still several years away. Aaron stood exactly six feet in height and weighed one hundred and ninety pounds. His short, sandy brown hair and clean shaven angular face seemed to be consistent with his trim figure and tan uniform. He liked to have his uniforms fitted, pressed and spotless. He also liked his shoes clean and his patrol car washed. He began several mornings a week with a three to four mile run and participated in 5K and 10K races on a regular basis. His work ethic and approach to the job had been molded by the chief. Aaron, having a great deal of respect for the chief, did not mind at all the usual comparisons. They did, however, have one major difference. Aaron, being single, enjoyed the social life. He liked meeting his buddies at

Ron's Bar and Grille and throwing back just a few beers and playing darts or pool. He also enjoyed deer hunting with a couple of his friends, an annual ritual which they looked forward to each year.

Chief Earl and Officer Aaron arrived at Stacy's house about ten minutes after receiving the call from Michelle. As they got out of their respective cars, the chief directed the officer to secure the perimeter of the scene, the house, as well as the entire property the house sat upon.

Stacy and her children continued to live in the house she and Shane had moved into when they first arrived back in Springerville. Shortly after the divorce, she had hired Josh to paint the exterior of the house. Per her instructions, he painted it an off-white color, with pink trim. She had always wanted pink trim, but Shane had absolutely refused. But now, the eves, window shutters, front door, front porch railing and window flower boxes, were all pink. Seasonal flowers were planted in all of the flower boxes and flower beds and were meticulously cared for. She paid one of the neighborhood boys to mow and trim her lawn every Saturday. She loved her home and had hoped to grow old right there, in her pretty little house, in her beloved Springerville.

Aaron opened his trunk from which he retrieved two rolls of police "do not cross" yellow ribbon and began to tie it from tree to tree around the property. Starting with the front yard, he quickly completed the border of the property, and then added additional tape to the front door and porch. As he approached the back porch, he couldn't help but stop and stare at the dead body of Stacy. It seemed surreal to him. For a moment, he just went numb: no thoughts, void of emotions, no moving, only staring. He decided to wait for the chief to come around before he taped off the porch and the door.

Meanwhile, the chief asked Josh where Stacy's body was located, asked a few quick questions, and then told Josh to stay on the front porch until he returned. He then walked around to the back of the house and looked at the body. He told Aaron to go get each of them a pair of latex gloves from his squad car. He slowly went up onto the porch and then carefully approached the body, making sure that each step did not land on any blood droplets or anything that might potentially be evidence. He approached her body, being certain to not step in the pool of blood. He held his index and middle fingers on the carotid artery to check for a pulse. He detected none. The body was cold to his touch, not extremely cold, just cold.

He did not immediately touch her again nor move her. He stood and then paused for a moment as he looked at Stacy's dead body, lying in a pool of her own blood. He took off his hat and lowered his head and closed his eyes as he thought, "What a terrible loss of such a young life." Saddened deeply, he couldn't help but reflect back on her as a teen and later as a newlywed. He would never have guessed that one day he would be standing over her dead body.

Two questions leapt to the forefront of his thoughts: "Why?" and "Will there be more?" The tragic scene only deepened his resolve to find the murderer and to find this person as quickly as possible.

He looked at the porch but did not see any bloody footprints nor any empty gun shells. On the porch were a small table with four chairs, a porch swing, her daughter's small bicycle with training wheels, and her son's Big Wheel. There were also a few toy trucks that her son had left in the corner of the patio. In the other corner was a large clay pot containing a small Ficus tree.

He looked at the doors and windows along the back of the house as well as along the side of the house as he returned to the front porch. Upon first inspection, no doors or windows appeared to be open or broken. The doors and windows along the front porch also showed no signs of a forced entry.

Aaron returned with the gloves and both he and the chief pulled them onto their hands as they returned to the back yard. The chief very carefully checked the back door and found it to be unlocked. He and Aaron entered slowly, being careful not to touch anything so as to preserve potential evidence. The back door opened into the kitchen, where they paused, looked around and then listened. They heard a noise, which they could not identify, coming from the other end of the house. They drew their weapons and slowly and quietly went from room to room, the chief stood at each door to watch the hallway, while Aaron checked closets, looked behind doors and under the beds, to be certain nobody was hiding.

They eventually got to the master bedroom, from which the noise appeared to be coming. The chief entered first, with Aaron following closely. They looked behind the door and then Aaron checked under the bed. They slowly made their way across the bedroom toward the walk-in closet, from where the noise was coming. However, they first had to walk past the master bathroom before they would reach the closet. The chief stood guard at the door of the bathroom, keeping his eye on the closet, while Aaron went into the bathroom to make sure that room was clear of any intruder. Aaron checked behind the door and then carefully and as quietly as he could, he opened the shower door. He found no one.

They carefully approached, then entered the closet. There, on a shelf at the back of the closet pointing toward the door, they found an old, worn out, oscillating fan, moving very slowly back and forth, making a slight clunking sound at one end of its swing. Stacy had purchased the old fan at a garage sale just a few months earlier because she thought the closet at times seemed stuffy and could us a little more air circulation. Aaron let out a long breath and looked at the chief. The chief, putting his revolver back in its holster, raised one eyebrow, tilted his head to one side, and shrugged his shoulders.

Not only did they not find anyone in the house, but neither did anything appear to be out of place or look peculiar in any way. They exited through the back door and walked around to the front porch.

As they approached Josh, the chief directed the officer to inspect the garage for any signs of forced entry or any other evidence. He then turned his attention to Josh.

He asked Josh how he was doing. Josh replied, "I guess I'm a little bit shaken up. I just can't believe it."

The chief asked if he'd like a glass of water. Josh said, "No, I'll be okay. I didn't know what to do so I called your office."

"You did the right thing," the chief assured him. Then the chief asked, "How long were you here before you called?"

"I called within a couple of minutes of finding her," Josh explained.

"Did you try to move her or revive her or touch her body at all?" the chief inquired.

"No," Josh quickly answered. "I saw all that blood and she was white as a sheet. I knelt down next to her and called her name a couple of times. Got no response. I assumed she was dead. Other than at a funeral or two, I've never seen a dead person. I started shaking like a leaf. So,

I came back to the front porch, sat down to catch my breath, and called Michelle at your office."

The chief then asked, "Why did you go to the back porch to begin with?"

Josh recounted his actions, "I was supposed to do a little repair work on the back porch. Some of the support beams were beginning to rot. We were going to replace some of the beams, railings and floorings. Some didn't need replaced, just repaired. Then we were going to paint the entire porch. I figured we could get the repair work done this morning and paint it this afternoon. When I arrived, I rang the doorbell, but nobody answered. Stacy knew I was coming today, so I figured I'd go around back and move some of the furniture and stuff off of the porch and then start moving my tools around to the back so we'd be ready to get started."

"You keep saying 'we.' Was Stacy planning on helping with this project?" asked the chief.

Josh shook his head and said, "No. Steve is supposed to be here. I guess he's running late, again."

The chief then asked, "Did you see any cars drive away when you pulled up?"

Josh said, "No."

The chief asked, "Did you see anyone else in the yard or walking down the street?"

Josh thought for a moment and then said, "I don't remember seeing anyone."

The chief continued, "Did you hear any voices or any noise from inside the house either before or after you rang the doorbell?"

Josh answered, "No voices, no noises."

"Okay," said the chief, "stick around just a little bit longer, would you please?"

"Sure thing," Josh replied.

Chapter Five: Looking For Evidence

The chief called and instructed Michelle to contact two other officers, Danielle Gilbert, who preferred her nickname, Dani, and Eric Good. Eric had been assigned radar patrol on the outskirts of town earlier that morning. He had already written two speeding tickets. One to a teen who was hurrying to school. The other to a guy from a different part of the state, on his way to a convention. He wasn't happy with the ticket and got a little mouthy with Eric. This caused Eric to take as long as he could to write the ticket. He also radioed Michelle to have her run a check on the plates, just because.

Dani was responding to a complaint from a couple who awoke to find toilet paper spread all over their yard. They had complained about the neighborhood kid playing loud music two nights earlier and felt that this TP job was a payback. Dani finished her report just as Michelle called. Michelle gave Dani the instructions from the chief, which included stopping by the station to pick up the crime investigation kit as well as the crime scene camera, and then to head on over to his location.

The chief had also instructed Michelle to contact Chaplain Bill Bergeson. Chaplain Bergeson was the pastor of a local congregation, but also served as the volunteer Chaplain for the police department. He and the chief had become good friends over the years and the chief had trusted and depended upon the Chaplain in some of the most difficult situations with which he had to deal. This was the worst of those situations.

Finally, the chief directed Michelle to call the morgue. They were to come and pick up the body and keep it at the morgue until the county coroner, Dr. Michael P. Terrace, could examine the body.

Eric arrived first, followed close behind by a reporter from the local newspaper, Mike Lambeau. Officer Aaron met them at the sidewalk and lifted the police tape as Eric ducked under and proceeded to the front porch. When

Mike began to follow, Aaron quickly stopped him and said, "Sorry, Mike. Not just yet."

"What's up?" Mike queried. "I heard on the scanner that the chief and you were here. And then he calls Eric and Dani in. Gotta be something big! What's happening?"

Aaron replied, "The chief will make a statement when he's ready. You're going to want to stick around. Hang tight."

A few neighbors began to gather around the front yard. They asked the officer and then the reporter what was going on. "All we can say at this time is that we are investigating a crime," Aaron explained. "The chief will release more information when appropriate to do so."

"Is Stacy okay?" someone asked loudly.

"I'm sorry," Aaron replied, "I cannot answer any questions nor give any information at this time. As soon as reasonably possible, the chief will make a statement." Aaron then joined the chief and other officers on the front porch.

At that moment, Dani arrived in her patrol car. Opening her truck, she grabbed the equipment needed and proceeded to the front porch. The chief instructed Dani to dust all doorknobs for finger prints, as well as any window latches which would be capable of holding a print. She was also to dust for prints all of the patio furniture on the back porch. Meanwhile, Eric was to take pictures of Stacy from all angles, as well as all angles of the back porch, house and yard. When he completed his task, Eric was instructed to cover Stacy's body.

Dani and Eric rounded the corner of the back yard at the same time and approached the porch. They stopped at the edge and took in the horrible scene. Eric took off his hat. Dani put her hand on Eric's arm. "This is terrible," she whispered. "Yeah," said Eric, not knowing what else to say. They both took a deep breath and then began the duties the chief had instructed them to do.

As soon as Eric and Dani had finished, and Eric had covered the body, the chief gathered his officers on the side of the house just as the chaplain arrived. After greeting the chaplain, Chief Earl took him to the edge of the back porch and waited as the chaplain took a moment to pray for Stacy, her children and her parents. He also prayed for guidance for the chief and his team during this investigation. Chief Earl quickly brought the chaplain up to speed on the little bit of information they had and then asked if he would visit Stacy's parents to give them the tragic news. He also asked the chaplain to explain that he would stop by their home later this morning, but that he could not possibly leave at this moment. The chaplain put his hand on the chief's shoulder, nodded, and then turned and walked away.

The chief then instructed Aaron to find Stacy's ex-husband, Shane, and break the news to him. This was the worst of many difficult assignments, but Aaron was the senior officer and knew implicitly that he was the logical one for the task. He walked briskly to his car, ignoring the many questions from the crowd, and drove away.

The chief then told the other two officers he was now going to make a statement to Mike and the rest of the small crowd, which was slowly growing out front. The officers were told to keep their eyes on the crowd as he announced what they had found.

As they approached the crowd, several asked what was going on and if Stacy was okay. Chief Earl held up his hands and said, "I'm sorry to have to tell you this, but Stacy has died."

There was a gasp from the crowd, and then Mike asked, "How did she die?"

"The cause of death has not yet been determined," the chief replied. "We've been here less than an hour and still have a lot of unanswered questions."

Mike pushed for more answers, "Was it a suicide, a murder, an accident?"

"That has not been determined," the chief said.

"Well, was there a suicide note?" Mike asked.

"I cannot give you any specifics about the case at this time," the chief insisted.

"Okay, then do you think it was a medical complication?" Mike probed.

"I cannot give you any specifics about the case at this time," the chief repeated.

"You keep going to the backyard. Is that where she died?" Mike continued.

"I cannot give you any specifics about the case at this time," the chief stated again.

"Is there anyone else in the house or in the backyard?" Mike persisted.

"MIKE, PLEASE!" the chief retorted. "We are way too early in our examination and investigation to answer any more questions. The cause of death has not been determined. As a matter of procedure, we will treat this as a crime scene until we get all of our questions answered."

But Mike wasn't yet finished, "Are there any weapons near the body? Is there any blood near the body? Is hers the only body found?"

The chief stared at Mike for a moment when he had finished, then slowly said, "Look Mike. I know you've got a job to do. I respect that. You're a good reporter. But I've also got a job to do. I simply will not give out speculative information. Furthermore, out of respect for her family, I will not make any further comment."

"One last question?" Mike persisted. The chief just looked at him.

Mike asked, "What about the family? Have they been notified yet?"

The chief took off his hat and ran his fingers through his hair. He explained, "Chaplain Bergeson is on his way to Stacy's folks' house to break the news to them. He will offer to stay with them at least until they are able to get Stacy's children from the school and bring them over there. Officer Aaron is on his way to find Shane and let him know what has happened. Please respect their privacy."

"Of course," Mike said quietly.

The chief then went back to the front porch, followed by both officers. He asked them, "Did you see any facial expressions or body language from those in the crowd that might cause you concern as they were told of Stacy's death?"

Dani replied, "It's hard to know what is a natural reaction, as opposed to an abnormal reaction, when hearing such horrible news. But I didn't see anything that looked really weird or extremely inappropriate."

Eric added, "I agree. No red flags."

The chief nodded and observed, "It was a long shot. But one never knows."

He then took the officers to the back porch and together they combed every inch of the porch, paying meticulous attention to the gaps between the planks, also looking beneath the porch, for any shell casings from a gun. They found none. They then stood shoulder to shoulder and worked their way back and forth across the yard, near the porch, looking for shell casings or any other evidence. Again, not a thing was found.

Eric asked, "Boss, why is looking for shell casings one of the first things we do? We don't even know if she was shot. Shouldn't we determine cause of death, first?"

The chief replied, "Men commit 90% of the murders in the U.S. Of those, 67% use a gun. We start with what is most likely. Also, I don't want to risk stepping on any shell casings and potentially contaminate evidence while trying to determine the cause of death. Patience and thoroughness are essential in investigating a crime scene."

"Does that mean you think she was shot?" Eric questioned.

"Nope. The evidence will tell us what to think. If she was murdered, she could have been shot, stabbed, beaten, hit with a blunt object, strangled or any number of other things. We also have to consider suicide. Slit wrists are what most suicide victims opt for, however, many also stab or cut their carotid artery, which, sadly, is much more effective and much quicker. That would certainly be consistent with the large pool of blood. Until we examine the body, we simply don't know. As I said, let the evidence speak."

"So, what do we do next?" Dani asked.

The chief nodded toward Stacy and said, "Now, it's time we turned her over."

Stacy had been laying front down, face turned to one side. They carefully uncovered her body and slowly rolled the body over onto her back. The wound was clearly seen and the cause of death became evident. All three focused their eyes upon a very large gash in her chest. Without moving her body again, the chief looked at her face, arms and the rest of her torso. He did not see any other wounds or markings.

"Evidently stabbed to death," the chief said. He then added, "Let's check the house for any weapon that could cause such a wound. Dani, you start in the kitchen. Eric, you search the two small bedrooms and the hallway bathroom. I'll search the master bedroom and bathroom and the living room. Aaron and I searched the house earlier, but we were looking for suspects. Let's do a detailed search for weapons or other evidence. Also, Eric, get a few more photos of Stacy now that we've turned her over. Make sure to include a close-up of the wound."

When the search of the house was competed, the three gathered again in the backyard. The chief said to his two officers, "No weapons found on the porch, the backyard, nor in the house. With no weapons nearby, obviously, this is not a self-inflicted wound. The evidence rules out suicide. This is now officially a murder investigation. But let's not say anything to anyone until the coroner does a complete examination."

At that moment two men from the local morgue arrived. After checking in with the chief, they brought a body bag and a gurney to the back porch. They placed Stacy's body in the bag and then lifted the bag onto the gurney. She was then wheeled to their hearse and placed inside, while the neighbors watched quietly, some crying. The hearse then left and took Stacy to the morgue, where it would wait the examination of Dr. Michael P. Terrace, county coroner.

The chief told Eric to give Aaron a call and give him an update on what they had discovered. He also instructed Eric and Dani to canvas the neighborhood, beginning with the crowd which had gathered out front, then door to door.

They were to ask if anyone had seen or heard anything that morning that could be relevant to the case. Afterward, they were to return to the station and fill out their reports. The chief then went over to talk to Josh.

Josh was still sitting on the front porch as he watched Stacy's body being loaded into the hearse and then watched the hearse drive slowly away. He lowered his head as tears ran down his cheeks and dropped to the ground. The chief approached him and asked if he was okay. Josh shrugged his shoulders and replied, "I guess so. Under the circumstances. Is it alright if I leave now?"

The chief said, "Is there anything else that comes to mind, anyone you might have seen or anything you might have seen, that you didn't remember earlier when we talked?"

Josh thought for a minute and said, "I'm sorry chief, I really wish I could tell you something to help. But I simply wasn't thinking about anything but this project as I pulled up. I just didn't pay much attention and I can't remember anything out of the ordinary."

The chief stated, "That's okay, Josh. But if you think of anything later, give me a call. Okay?"

Josh replied, "Yes, I will."

"One more thing," the chief added. "I thought you said that Steve was going to meet you here. Any idea where he is?"

Josh looked puzzled, and then said, "I have no idea."

Chapter Six: Two Friends

Steve Winter and Josh Allen had been friends since childhood. In high school, they would go to school dances together and eventually double dated. When they were younger they had done a lot of fishing, hunting and camping together with their dads. As they got older, they went on their own. Their last two years of high school, Josh was always with the love of his life, Andrea. Steve had a big crush on Stacy, as had several other boys over the years. He even dated her several times during their first two years in high school. But then along came Shane, and Steve was history. He dated several other girls while in high school and after. He had even lived with one or two since high school, but never settled down and married. Josh always felt that Stacy had broken Steve's heart and he had never completely recovered.

Josh could not imagine ever being restricted to an office job. He loved being outside; preferably camping, fishing or hunting. He therefore chose a career which would not restrict him to being "caged in an office," as he referred to it. He stood five feet eight inches tall and had short, sandy brown hair. He felt that shaving was an unnecessary evil and thus a razor rarely touched his face.

While Josh was at trade school, Steve was working with a construction framing crew. Once Josh got his business up and running, he needed help occasionally on large projects. Steve would help him if his crew was between jobs or he'd help after work or on weekends. Eventually Josh hired him full time. Steve jumped at the job offer. Not only did it pay better than what he was making as a framer, but he enjoyed working with Josh as well as liked having a variety of jobs instead of the same ol' same ol' every day. Steve had proven to be a very hard and reliable worker, and the two got along great, most of the time.

Occasionally, Steve would want to grab a beer after work, but Josh wanted to get home to his family. Steve would grumble and complain, Josh would just laugh it off and head home. Once in a while they would stop by the local tavern for a quick brewsky, but home is where Josh preferred to be. Steve accepted this, in fact, was somewhat jealous, but he treasured Josh's friendship and thus enjoyed the times they did stop for a drink, a game of pool and the usual sarcastic banter.

Josh got up from the porch and walked toward his truck. Mike stopped him as soon as he ducked under the yellow police ribbon and approached his truck.

"Hey, Josh. Can I ask you a few questions?" Mike asked.

"Not now, Mike. Maybe later," Josh responded.

Mike persisted, "Common Josh, it'll just take a minute."

"Sorry man. Chief Earl told me not to talk to anyone about anything that happened here this morning. Can't help you," Josh replied.

"Hey, I'm just trying to do my job," Mike lamented

Josh said, "I understand. Still, no comment."

"Maybe later?" Mike pleaded.

"Maybe," Josh steadfastly said.

At that moment Steve came cruising up on his motorcycle. He stopped the bike, got off, and looked around in wonderment.

As he approached Josh and Mike he asked, "What the hell's going on? I saw a hearse driving by up around the corner. Police tape, cop cars, Mike." Then he quipped, "What did you do this time, Josh?!"

"Not funny," Josh answered.

"Okay, then what's up?" Steve continued.
Josh looked at Mike and said, "Can you give us a minute?"

Mike answered, "Sure. I'm going down to the police station to see if I can get any more info. But I'm going to call you later, we'll talk then."

"Well, we'll see," said Josh. Then he turned to Steve, looked around at a couple of the neighbors standing nearby and said, "Get into the truck."

"What? Why?" Steve questioned.

"Just shut up and get in the truck," Josh said as he went to the driver's side of the truck, opened the door and slid in. Steve went to the passenger door and got in.

"Okay. NOW can you tell me what in the world is going on?" Steve demanded.

"Stacy's dead. I found her laying on the back porch when I arrived this morning. The chief's been here, officers have been here, the morgue guys have been here. She's dead, man!"

Steve sat in silence, speechless. He turned his head and stared out the windshield.

"But that's not all," Josh added. "They think she was murdered. They haven't officially announced it yet, but I heard the chief talking to the officers. He told them that she was murdered."

"Murdered!?" Steve said. "How do they know that? Do they know who did it?"

"No. They don't know anything yet. Just that there was a lot of blood. It was terrible," Josh explained.

"Wow," Steve said as he slowly exhaled.

"That's all you've got to say? Wow." Josh steamed.

"What are you mad at me about? I didn't kill her," Steve pleaded.

"I didn't say you did. But where in the hell have you been for the last two hours? You're late, if you haven't noticed," Josh fumed.

Steve said, "I, uh, er, I, I overslept. My alarm didn't go off. I was up late last night, had a few drinks, went to bed. I guess I had more than a few. Forgot to set my alarm. Sorry, man. No big deal. As I was riding over, I planned to work a couple hours extra to make up for it. But what does that have to do with anything anyway. I was late. Big deal. These things happen."

"These things happen? Like murder? Murder just happens? That's what you're saying?" Josh demanded.

"No! Not murder. Oversleeping. Late for work. That happens sometimes," Steve quickly explained.

Josh said, "Well, you picked a hell of a day to just happen to be late."

"Hey, Josh. Look, I'm sorry. Obviously I didn't know. Okay. I'm sorry." Steve replied.

Josh let out a long sigh, and said, "Well. It doesn't matter now. No work today. I've got to go home and tell Andrea what happened. I'll call you later today."

Steve started to get out of the truck. Then he stopped and said, "Do you mind if I come over and just kind of hang out with you two for a while? This may sound strange, but I don't want to go home to an empty house. You know, it's all just kind of weird."

Josh thought for a minute and then said, "Sure, of course you can. But give me a few minutes to talk to Andrea before you get there, okay?"

Steve said, "Thanks boss. I'll swing by Truman's and get some bagels and coffee."

Josh answered, "Sounds good. Take your time."

"Will do," Steve replied

Josh watched as Steve climbed onto his motorcycle and slowly drove away. He listened to the distinct guttural, deep throated sound of the Harley. Josh thought to himself, "Good thing he added those hard case saddle bags on the back. Otherwise, he wouldn't be able to carry my coffee ..."

Chapter Seven: Messenger of Death

Chief Earl returned to the station. He then told Michelle that he was going to visit Stacy's parents. After that visit, he planned to track down Richard White and have a discussion with him.

When Chief Earl paid his visit to Stacy's parents, Chaplain Bergeson was still there. The chief extended his condolences and, after many tears, they began to ask a series of questions. He tried to answer as many questions as possible, but they had more questions than he had answers. He assured them that he would do his absolute best to find the individual who had done this to their daughter.

From there, the chief drove to Richard's office. Richard was busy on the phone, apparently with a client. His demeanor suggested to the chief that he had not yet heard the news about Stacy. Once off the phone, the secretary ushered the chief into Richard's office and closed the door as she left.

Richard was an insurance agent who had moved to Springerville about eight years ago. After Shane and Stacy had divorced, Stacy had dated several other men. Most recently she had been dating Richard, who was six years older than Stacy. Those who knew them did not expect this latest relationship to last very long. They often argued when together and complained about each other when apart. Yet, they continued in their relationship. Perhaps, because neither liked the idea of being alone. Stacy's children did not like Richard, and they made no secret of their dislike of him. The feeling was mutual. Richard could not help feel that he was constantly competing with her children for Stacy's time and attention. It was just another in several of their ongoing arguments.

His biggest frustration was Stacy's refusal to move in together. He thought that two years of dating was long enough, and that neither was in the financial position to waste money on two living locations. She had the house, which she got in her divorce, along with the mortgage payment, that her parents assisted with. He rented an apartment and felt that the rent and utilities expense could be saved if they both lived in her house. But she refused. And they argued. Yet, they stayed together.

When the chief arrived, Richard was in a suit and tie, which he always wore when working. Richard believed that professionals should dress like professionals and always dressed appropriately for work as well as any professional functions or social events. His distinguished dark hair, graying at the temples, seemed to accent his stylish dress. He was very involved in the Chamber of Commerce and enjoyed being on the mayor's task force to promote local businesses.

Richard was somewhat of a newcomer to the town of Springerville. He not only was from out of town, he was from out of state. He had married immediately out of high school but realized quickly that neither he nor his wife were ready to settle down. They divorced amicably and remained somewhat friends the next few years.

During this time, Richard had become an insurance agent and had done well for himself. He wasn't getting rich, but he was paying his bills. He was somewhat frugal and careful not to waste money on too many of what he called, "unnecessary encumbrances."

Eventually his insurance company informed him that one of their agents in another town would soon be retiring and they were looking for an agent to take over his business. It was much different than what Richard was used to. He had been working in an office with several agents, so this would be a new experience – running a one agent office in a small town. Richard liked the idea as well as the challenge, pursued the new opening, and eventually ended up working in Springerville.

He made friends quickly and became involved in the business community. He worked hard, was efficient and quickly made a good name as well as a good reputation for himself. He had been there for about six years when he began dating Stacy Pruitt.

As the chief entered the office, Richard stood and smiled, they shook hands, and then both were seated.

"To what do I owe the pleasure of your visit, Chief Earl?" Richard quipped.

The chief said, "This time it's strictly business, Richard. By that I mean police business, not insurance business. Let me ask a quick question, how have you and Stacy been getting along lately?"

Richard seemed somewhat surprised by the bluntness of the question, but he knew the chief to be a no-nonsense kind of guy, so he was quick to reply, "To be honest with you, there are times that woman drives me crazy. We've gone through some rough patches, but we still have our great moments, too."

"When was the last time you two were together?" the chief continued. The chief noticed that Richard paused for just a moment before answering.

"We had lunch together yesterday. Why do you ask? Chief, what's going on!?" Richard demanded.

The chief cleared his throat and said, "There's no easy way to say this. I'm sorry, but I have some very bad news. Stacy was found dead this morning."

"What! Found dead?! What do you mean? Where, when, how? Are you sure?" Richard stammered.

"Unfortunately, yes. I'm sure. She was found on her back porch by Josh Allen when he went there to do some repair work for her," the chief stated.

"Dead? But … how, why, what happened?" questioned Richard.

The chief said, "We are not sure why. We don't know for sure how it happened. But, we believe she was murdered. She's at the morgue now, waiting for the coroner's examination."

"Murdered?! You've got to be kidding me. Who in the world would do such a thing? That can't be right. Not Stacy. Everyone loved Stacy. Chief Earl, are you sure you've got all your facts right?" Richard asked.

"We certainly don't have all the facts. We're still putting the pieces together. We haven't announced that yet, but that is certainly what it looks like at this time and that is how we are investigating it at this time. Tell me Richard, can you think of anyone who would want to hurt Stacy?" asked the chief.

"Absolutely not. Not a chance. There's got to be a lot more to this story!" Richard stated.

"I'm sure there is, Richard, I'm sure there is. But for now, that's all we've got." The chief paused for a moment, thinking, and then said to Richard, "There's a few more questions I need to ask you, but out of respect for your loss and understanding the grief you are now dealing with, we'll wait to ask those questions."

Richard looked blankly at the chief and just nodded.

The chief concluded, "I'm sorry to have to bring you this tragic news. I'll keep you in the loop as the investigation continues. Either Aaron or I will get back to you," the chief said as he dismissed himself and got up to leave.

"Thanks chief," Richard murmured.

The chief closed the door as he left. Richard sat at his desk for a few minutes, in a daze, unable to believe what he had just been told. Then he lowered his head and cried.

Meanwhile, Officer Aaron had just pulled into the school parking lot when he received the call from Officer Eric with the updated information from the crime scene. He then went to the school office to find out where on the campus Shane was at that time. Shane had just started his third hour P.E. class when Aaron tracked him down and told him he had an emergency and would need someone to cover the class for him. Another teacher was summoned from the teacher's lounge, was given some quick instructions for the class and then Aaron and Shane went into the coach's office.

As soon as they sat down, Aaron said, "Shane, I have some tragic news for you. Stacy was found dead this morning. Josh Allen was going to do some repair work on her back porch and found her there. She had been dead for a little while."

Shane just sat, stunned, without saying a word. He stared at Aaron in disbelief. He then looked at the ground with a quizzical expression, as if trying to figure out what exactly he had heard. But Aaron had been straight forward, very to the point, and there was no mistaking what he had just been told. He looked up at Aaron, but still was unable to speak.

Then, his eyes opened wide and he blurted out, "What about my kids?!"

Aaron answered, "The kids are okay. They had spent the night at Stacy's parents' house and had gone straight to school from there. They have been taken from school back over to Stacy's parents."

Aaron continued, "Stacy has been taken to the morgue. Her parents and the kids have been told. You probably should head over there to be with them."

Shane, as if in a mental fog, said, "Yes. Sure. Of course. I'll go right now." Then he paused and added, "But Aaron, how did she die? What happened?"

Aaron cleared his throat and then said, "Shane. We're just not sure yet. We need to wait for the coroner's report. I'm not even sure what I'm allowed to say at this point. But it's not good."

Shane demanded, "What do you mean, 'not good?' Did she overdose? Did she take her own life? What the hell does 'not good' mean?"

In frustration, Aaron explained, "Okay. I'm going to tell you something, but I'm not sure if I'm supposed to say this just yet. But, you're going to hear it real quick anyway. So for now, this is just between you and me. We think that Stacy was murdered."

"Murdered? By who? Why do you think she was murdered? Come on Aaron, you're talking about my ex-wife, the mother of my children. Please, tell me what you know!" Shane demanded.

Aaron quickly responded, "I've told you everything I know, Shane. Josh found her on the back porch, in a puddle of blood. There's no evidence the house was broken into. Nothing was stolen. No weapons laying around. So far, nobody saw anything or heard anything. Right now, we've got absolutely nothing to go on. I'm sorry, but that's all I've got."

Shane continued, "Blood!? Where did the blood come from? Was she shot? Did you see her before they took her to the morgue?"

Aaron squirmed a little in his seat, not sure how much detail he should give. Then he tried to explain, "There was a wound in her chest. We don't know what caused the wound or who caused it. The blood came from that wound. As far as we can tell, there are no other wounds. That's honestly all we know. There's really nothing more I can say, other than, I'm so very sorry to have to bring you this horrible news."

Shane was again silent for a moment. Then, the tears came. "This just doesn't make sense. This can't be happening. This is crazy," Shane sobbed.

Aaron waited for a few minutes and then offered to give Shane a ride over to Stacy's parents so he could be with his children. Shane replied that he needed to let the principle and Coach Stewart know what was going on, and then he'd drive himself over because he needed his car to get home later. Aaron told him that he'd inform the principle and the coach, so that Shane could get over to where he needed to be. Shane thought for a minute, then nodded and thanked Aaron for letting the others know. He then picked up his keys and walked out to his car.

Just two years after their daughter was born, Shane and Stacy had their second child, a little boy, whom they named Kolton. As might be expected, the gifts at the baby shower, toys and clothes, all had a sports theme. Mostly football. Stacy was a stay at home mom and Shane continued to teach and coach at the high school. Most thought Stacy was living the Cinderella story with the happy ending, but such was not the case.

Her major frustration was that Shane was, in her words, always gone. He was, of course, at school during the day and then stayed after school coaching one team or another. He then would return to his classroom to grade papers or prepare for the next day's classes. When Stacy would ask why he couldn't do the prep work at home or even during his free hour during the day, he explained that between all the interruptions from her and the kids, he couldn't ever get any work done at home.

When he wasn't coaching various sports teams, he was out playing on a variety of sports teams. Although he had to wear a knee brace to support his injured knee, he was still very competitive and did well in his various sporting activities. Sometimes informal pick-up games of basketball down at the gym, other times in the city softball league. He even joined a coed bowling league, in which Stacy had no interest in participating.

To further her frustration, it was not uncommon for him to join the guys at Ron's Bar and Grille for a few drinks after whichever activity they were involved. The little bit of time they were home was mostly spent arguing. On more than one occasion, when he got home very late after spending the evening at Ron's Bar and Grille, she stated that womanizing had become one of his sports. While he vehemently denied the accusation, she wasn't always wrong.

Ultimately, most were not surprised when they divorced after seven and a half years of marriage. She kept the house and received child support and alimony. He moved into an apartment near the high school. He would visit the kids on weekends, when not too busy with other activities. His time with the kids, or lack thereof, became their new source of argument. The idolized "All-American couple" never lived up to their perfect image. Not even close. And now, Stacy was dead.

Officer Aaron went to the principal's office, Randy Pace, and filled him in on the news and answered a barrage of questions as best he could. Principal Pace called Coach Stewart into his office and Aaron repeated the entire process.

To say that Coach Stewart was "old school" would be a tremendous understatement. His hair style, if it can be called that, was a short cropped flat top, completely gray. It was, in fact, the only hair style he had his entire life. Some said he had the face of a bulldog and a body to match. He carried his 245 pounds on a five foot eight inch frame. His stout arms and legs were overshadowed by a very firm and large gut. Beer was his beverage of choice. He usually had two or three bottles while enjoying a nice cigar, sitting on his back porch in the cool of the evening. He would never drink nor smoke around the youngsters. But, when alone with a couple of coaches in his own backyard, which happened often, two or three beers and a stogie were the norm.

When with his coaching buddies, they of course talked about sports, mostly football. After discussing their local high school team, the coach would also enjoyed talking about his favorite collegiate team, the University of Michigan Wolverines. In the cool of the evening he typically would wear an old, worn out blue sweatshirt with a big yellow M on the front. He had never played at Michigan, nor did he attend Michigan, but having grown up in

Kalamazoo, Michigan, he had been a Wolverine fan since childhood. He had fond memories of the teams led by Bo Schembechlar who had coached the Wolverines for 21 years. His coaching buddies loved to tease him about his hero, reminding him that Bo had never won a national championship and had an abysmal 2-8 record in the Rose Bowl, including a big upset loss to Arizona State in 1987. When they really wanted to get under his skin, they would talk about the superiority of The Ohio State Buckeyes and their recent dominance of the Wolverines. This inevitably lead to increase in the swearing and name calling as the trash talking, laughter and drinking continued into the evening. On his most recent birthday, one of his assistant coaches gave Coach Stewart an Ohio State Buckeyes jersey for his birthday gift. This led to profane laced comments by the coach about the assistant coach's family lineage, the legitimacy of his birth, his intelligence, his looks and any other derogatory comments Coach Stewart could come up with. This, of course, led to great laughter from the other coaches present, and another round of beers.

As a football coach, Coach Stewart believed in discipline and fundamentals. He preferred the run over the pass, but did open up the passing game if the talent of his quarterback warranted it. Of course, when Shane played for him, he was able to set school records in passing attempts, passing completions, total yards passing in a game, total yards passing in a season, touchdowns by pass in both game and season ... in fact, most of the passing records on the books for Springerville High School eventually were held by Shane Pruitt. Of course they also ran the ball. But while Shane was the quarterback, the run was only to set up the pass. Shane's senior year they won their conference and set their sights on a state title. Unfortunately, they lost a very close, high scoring game in regional play. No one was more heartbroken over that defeat than Shane and his coach.

Coach Stewart was a very strong disciplinarian. The team ran wind sprints until they thought their legs would fall off. He blew his whistle often and screamed at players regularly throughout practice as well as during games. The guys who played on Coach Stewart's team did so with pride. Sure he was tough, but to be on his team gave you instant respect, not only at school but in the community as well. Those who played for Coach Stewart were part of a special fraternity. Many stayed right in Springerville after graduation and attended the Friday night games every fall. The former players had a bond that was easily recognized in the small community. It was like a close nit family. The head of that family was, of course, Coach Stewart.

There was no secret that Shane was the all-time favorite player Coach Stewart ever had on one of his Springerville High School football teams. Upon hearing of Shane's knee injury, the coach was devastated. It was great consolation, to both, when Shane was hired and returned to the high school. The coach and his favorite player were being reunited again, and both were pleased.

Upon hearing the tragic news of Stacy's death, the principal had been shocked and sad, but then very professional and all business. He talked about giving Shane time off and lining up substitutes. Coach Stewart was also shocked and sad, but he was also very angry. The more questions he asked, the madder he seemed to get, in spite of the answers Aaron provided.

Finally, the coach blurted out, "The worst thing that ever happened to Shane was getting mixed up with that girl. He was a superstar! With all of their constant bickering and fighting, it's no wonder he could never keep his mind on coaching our team. Coaches work long hours. We study game film. We strategize a plan for the next team we face. We constantly evaluate our own players. Shane was a great player and still has a chance to be a great coach. But he had to constantly worry about his kids and who little miss Stacy was dating this time. If she had made their marriage work, maybe none of this would have happened!"

Both the principal and Aaron sat astonished and stunned at the coach's outburst. At first, neither said a word.

Aaron thought to himself, "If SHE had made their marriage work?! Wow."

Then, the principal said calmly and slowly, "Coach, this is an extremely tragic and emotional bit of news we have just received. We will want to be very careful to not let our emotions say something rash or something we'll later regret having said."

The coach still seemed to seethe with anger while staring at the principal. He then looked at Aaron and then back to the principal. He stood up, walked over to the wall, and then returned to the chair and sat down. He then stammered, "You're right. I'm sorry. Please ignore what I just said. Tragic. It's all just so tragic. And so, unnecessary."

All three sat in silence for a brief moment, and again it was the principle who spoke first. He said, "Coach, I'm going to give Shane some time off. Can you get some of the guys to cover his P.E. classes and coaching duties. I'll line up some substitute teachers for his math classes."

"Yeah. Sure. I'll take care of it right now," the coach said as he stood up and walked out of the room.

Aaron looked at the principal and said, "That was intense."

"Indeed" the principal answered.

With that, Aaron thanked the principle, stood and walked out to his squad car.

Chapter Eight: Work The Case

Dani Gilbert had grown up in a police family. Her father was a career police officer and both of her brothers were also cops. At first, Dani struggled with going into police work. She didn't want to enter that career just because her father and brothers had done so. She didn't want to do so because others expected her to. Nor did she want to do so to prove to some of the antagonists that a female could do just as well as a male could do as an officer. No, her reasons were of a higher level, perhaps more altruistic.

She simply believed in what police work stands far. Police are the ones who protect the good guys from the bad guys. They are the ones who are there in someone's time of need. They are the final line of defense when a community or society teetered on the brink of chaos. They are to protect and serve. Deep down, she believed that police officers, fire fighters, military and teachers were the true heroes of society. In her mind, it was a high calling, one that, ultimately, she embraced wholeheartedly.

Dani ultimately decided that although she would follow in the career path of her father and brothers, she would not follow that path into the same police department the three of them were in. She didn't want to have to deal with the comparisons or expectations and certainly not the potential accusations of nepotism. So, upon her graduation from the academy, when she heard that Springerville was looking to add a new officer, she applied and was hired by Chief Earl.

Standing five feet six inches tall, with long black hair and brilliant blue eyes, her unassuming personality betrayed her strikingly beautiful looks. Having had two older brothers, she was used to teasing and being teased, and she could dish it out just as well as she could take it. She was quick to laugh, at herself as well as with others. Her laughing and teasing was most pronounced when she was around Eric Good. In this regards, they were very similar: teasing, pranks, laughing, telling jokes, they had become good friends in the two and a half years they had worked together. Additionally, they were both excellent officers. They took their jobs very seriously and were constantly looking for ways to learn and improve as officers. Both of them held Chief Earl in high regard and enjoyed being a part of the small police department in Springerville.

They also quickly learned that their shenanigans, or "horseplay" as Chief Earl referred to it, were not to be done while he was around, and certainly never during a meeting which involved discussion of the job. Not that he, himself, didn't poke fun at his friends. But there was a time and a place for everything, and on this issue, the chief determined the time and the place.

As Eric and Dani began to canvas the neighborhood, they agreed to split up, each taking opposite sides of the street. As they got started, Dani teased, "Make sure you take a map and compass so you don't get lost!"

"Hardy-har-har," Eric replied.

"Oh, great comeback. I bet you were up all night thinking that one up," Dani continued.

Eric countered, "Just be sure to show your badge, so they don't think you're out selling Girl Scout cookies."

"Hardy-har-har back at 'cha," Dani reciprocated.

"Very original," Eric quipped, then turned and walked up the walkway of the first house.

They spent the rest of the morning and into the afternoon canvassing the neighborhood. They both enjoyed being outside on this beautiful fall day. Eric looked up to watch a flock of geese flying south. He had seen this same sight hundreds of times but still enjoyed their V-formation and the distinct honking as they flew. Dani enjoyed the beautiful fall colors of the leaves on the large Birch, Maple, Oak, and Dogwood trees which were found in most of the yards. She especially enjoyed the various fruit trees, Apple, Pear, and Cherry, which a few of the yards had. She saw a swing hanging from a low tree branch in two of the yards and a small treehouse in another. Many of the homes had a small picket fence or a small hedge around their yard. Most of the homes were well maintained and cared for, although a few were in need of a fresh coat of paint. A small front porch was also common on most of the homes.

When the officers had finished canvasing the neighborhood, they met back in front of Stacy's house. Dani was there a few minutes before Eric completed his side of the street.

"Took you long enough," Dani teased. "Did you stop for lunch?"

"Nope. But I was offered some homemade cookies at one house and some peanut butter fudge at another. It would have been rude of me to decline," Eric said with a big grin.

"Did you bring any back for your partner," Dani asked, already knowing the answer.

"Of course not," Eric said. Then not wanting to miss an opportunity for a quick jab, he added, "I was only thinking of your diet. It would be terrible if you had to tell the chief that you could no longer fit into your uniform."

"Speaking of which," Dani responded, "have you stepped on the scales lately?"

"Ouch!" Eric said, laughing. Then he continued, "Seriously, any luck with the canvasing?"

"Possibly," Dani answered, "Mrs. Simmons saw Dr. Clevenger walking his dog. Mr. Bates saw a motorcycle drive by. He said that he was pretty certain that it was a Harley, because of the sound. He then added that he thought it was that, 'Steve Winter kid.'"

Eric laughed and said, "Kid?! I'm pretty sure he's older than I am!"

Dani grinned and said, "Yeah, I thought that was pretty funny. I guess 'kid' is a relative term, once you're retired! Anyway, he didn't know what time it went by, just that it was early. Other than that, a few people saw the school bus come down the street, saw the paper boy ride by on his bike, heard a few cars come and go and a couple of dogs barking. But nothing out of the ordinary. At three of the houses no one answered the door bell. I rang the bell a second time and knocked, I guess they weren't home."

Eric replied, "I may have a lead. At first I was getting pretty much what you have. But, I only had one house with no one home. Most everyone said pretty much the same thing, typical morning stuff. Up at the other end of the street, Mr. & Mrs. Montgomery said they saw Dr. Clevenger talking to an older lady in an old green car. They couldn't say who the lady was and couldn't tell what make or model the car was, just old and green. And of course, no chance they'd remember a plate number. They said the conversation only lasted a couple of minutes, and then the car headed down this way, toward Main Street."

Dani, acting as if she were deep in thought said, "Hmmm. Let me see. An old lady in an old green car, very early in the morning, last seen heading toward Main Street. No doubt, on her way to back over a fire hydrant."

Eric smiled and said, "I'm thinking old lady Perkins may have still been thinking about Dr. Clevenger when she should have been thinking about parallel parking."

Dani laughed, and then replied, "And, that's your big lead?"

"Not at all, Sherlock, get this," Eric explained. "At the corner, I talked with a Mr. & Mrs. Luker. They were of course shocked to hear about Stacy. Didn't see or hear anything this morning, but then she said they had seen Stacy at dinner last night."

"Really?" Dani observed. "Was she with anyone?"

"Indeed she was," Eric explained. "Richard White. But wait until you hear this. They were having an argument. They said it got so intense that Stacy got up and walked out. Didn't even finish her food. Left Richard just sitting there, fuming."

"Wow, looks like you just stumbled upon our first lead. Good job, officer!" Dani commented.

"Stumbled nothing. That's just outstanding detective work," Eric enthused.

"Of course, because it's so difficult to knock on a door, at the boss's instruction, and ask a few questions. At least you didn't get lost walking down the street," Dani teased.

"Stick around girly, you might just learn a few things," Eric quipped.

"If so, it certainly won't be a lesson in humility. More like a lesson in how to mooch cookies and fudge from unsuspecting citizens," responded Dani.

Eric smiled again as he said, "Sounds like someone might be just a little bit jealous."

Dani just shook her head and said, "We better get back to the station, the boss will want to hear about this. And seriously, good job."

As he stepped over to his squad car, Eric said, "Thanks. See you there."

But, before either could get into their patrol cars, a car pulled up in front of them. Dotty Miller quickly jumped out of the car, sobbing, and hurried toward them. The officers looked at each other, and then Dani stepped forward.

Dotty grabbed Dani's arm and cried, "I just heard the terrible news. Please tell me it isn't true. Please tell me Stacy is okay. Please tell me she isn't ... gone."

Dani responded, "Dotty, I'm sorry, I wish I could tell you something different. But the truth is, Stacy died this morning. The chief was here earlier. So was Officer Aaron. Eric and I have been interviewing people in the neighborhood. We don't know a lot just yet. But what you've heard is true, sad as it is."

Dotty began to sob horribly as she clung to Dani. Dani just hugged her and gave her time. Eric walked over and put his hand on her shoulder. Dotty turned and hugged Eric, then reached into her purse to get a couple of tissues to dry her eyes and clean up some of the mascara running down her cheeks.

Eric looked at Dani, and Dani nodded. Eric then said to Dotty, "If you are okay, we'd like to ask you a few questions."

Dotty looked at him and then at Dani. She then looked back at Eric and said, "What kind of questions?"

Eric said, "Just some simple questions we've been asking people in the neighborhood. And a few questions about Stacy, what's been going on in her life. That kind of stuff."

Dotty thought for a minute and then shook her head, "I just can't right now. She's my best friend. I just found out. I need some time."

"I understand," Eric said. "Perhaps later this evening or maybe tomorrow."

"Yes," she said, "Maybe tomorrow. Do you know where her kids are? Those poor darlings."

Dani explained, "Michelle radioed me a few minutes ago and said that Kortnee and Kolton are at Stacy's parents' house. Shane is also over there."

"I need to get over there," Dotty sounded urgent as she said it.

"Of course," said Dani, "We'll contact you tomorrow."

Dotty hurried to her car, got in and quickly drove away. Dani looked at Eric and said, "Word is spreading quickly."

Eric replied, "Yes it is. There are going to be a lot of shocked and very sad people in this town." She nodded and then each went to their patrol car and drove back to the station. They began filling out their reports, the tedious part of the job most of the public never sees. Shortly thereafter, the Chief and Aaron both returned.

Eric had been hired by Chief Earl about six months after Dani had been hired. She took great pleasure in constantly reminding him that she was the senior officer of the two. He was the fourth of six children in his family. He was five feet ten inches tall, broad shouldered and barrel chested. His powerful arms were like a set of mighty pistons. In high school he was a linebacker on the football team and was division champion in his weight class on the wrestling team. He still holds his high school's record for the amount of weight lifted in the bench press. In college, he tried boxing for a while. He enjoyed it, and did well in the few matches in which he participated, but had other interests that he eventually pursued.

Since childhood, as long as he can remember, he wanted to be a cop. When the kids in the neighborhood played cops and robbers, he had to be a cop, or he simply wouldn't play. He couldn't even comprehend playing the role of a robber. He detested the nickname, "Red," especially when attached to his name, as in Eric the Red. Many were quick to try to give him this moniker because of his thick, red hair. As an adult he either ignored the nickname or politely informed the person that Red wasn't his name. As a child, if a kid in the neighborhood used it, he replied with an uppercut to the kid's chin.

His temperament was somewhat a paradox, in that, he was a happy-go-lucky individual most the time. He loved to laugh and tease and pull pranks on a regular basis. He was everybody's buddy and enjoyed meeting strangers. But he also had a very explosive fuse. He very rarely lost his temper, but when he did, it was no small issue. As a child, this got him into trouble many times. As an adult, especially working as a cop, he had learned to control his temper. He could take verbal abuse all day long, and even some physical abuse, to a point, and maintain his calm. But if anyone harmed someone he cared about, all bets were off. He considered his fellow officers to be family. As such, he had their back, always.

When all of the officers had returned to the station, they quickly assembled in the conference room and while going over their notes, each shared what they had discovered thus far. The chief directed Michelle to call Dr. Terrace at the coroner's office and ask when the report on Stacy would be ready.

After sharing information and answering questions, Chief Earl gave further instructions. "Okay, first thing in the morning and we'll start doing some follow-up. Finish your reports today, make sure everything is documented. You know the routine. Also, try to wrap up anything else you have on your plate. Obviously, this is priority number one. Tomorrow morning, we hit the ground running. We want absolute thoroughness, due diligence, in everything."

"Keep in mind motive and opportunity. In regards to motive, women are most often killed by their husband or boyfriend, or by their ex-husband or former boyfriend. That puts Richard White and Shane Pruitt at the top of our list.

In regards to opportunity, Steve Winter appears to have been at the right place at the right time."

The chief continued, "Aaron, I want you to follow-up on Richard White. I didn't want to be insensitive and hit him with a lot of tough questions within minutes of informing him that his girlfriend had just been murdered. But there are questions that need to be asked because there are all kinds of red flags here. He was in a relationship with her which was strained, at best. They were seen by witnesses having an argument at dinner the night before, but told me the last time he saw her was at lunch. Find out why he lied, find out what they were arguing about, and find out where he was early this morning. If necessary, bring him in for further questioning."

"Aaron, I also want you to pay Coach another visit. The little outburst you described that he had needs to be probed a bit. His temper might be a problem. Probably another long shot, but as I said, due diligence."

He then turned to Eric. "Shane presents a challenge. Ex-husband, but we know of no recent conflicts between the two. Right now he's got to be overwhelmed with the thought of raising those two children by himself. That prospect by itself works against the motive angle. Still, he needs to be considered. Don't contact him directly just yet, but see if you can find out where he was early this morning. Also, I'll need you to handle any calls that come in tomorrow. Prioritize. If you need any help, let Michelle know and she'll contact one of us."

"Along that line, I've contacted the County Sheriff and he is going to send a deputy down to help with our work load for a few days. That will help free up some time to focus on this case. He'll send more if needed, if things get crazy."

"Also, I want to develop a time line for everything that happened on Stacy's street this morning. Dani, call Dr. Clevenger and Mrs. Perkins to see what time they had their conversation as well as what time the motorcycle drove by. Let Eric know what you find out. Eric, ask

Michelle to check her phone log to determine the exact time Josh called in this morning when he found Stacy's body. I'll find out from Josh what time he actually arrived on the site. Review all of the reports you and Dani took when you canvassed the neighbors. Anything that can be nailed down to a time, include in the time line. Understand?"

"Absolutely. I'll get right on it," Eric said enthusiastically.

The chief continued, "Dani, I want you to talk to Dotty Miller. Don't take no for an answer. You can give her until late morning before you contact her. We've got to be sensitive, but one of these people might very well be Stacy's murderer, or at least know something relevant to the case. Sensitive but firm. That's our mantra on this one. While waiting to set up your meeting with her, let's confirm the Dr. Clevenger story."

Dani, with raised eyebrow asked, "Dr. Clevenger? Really?"

"Yep," the chief replied. "I know. Not likely. But he was on the street, seen by a couple of people, perhaps at the time of the murder. He had opportunity. I'll say it again, due diligence. Leave no stone unturned. No surprises. Talk with him and with Anne Perkins. Make sure that whole story checks out."

To all three he said, "Clues aren't found under a flashing neon sign that says, 'clues located here.' Be alert. Work the case. No shortcuts. Stacy deserves our best effort. Together, we're going to solve this. Remember the two important keys: Motive and opportunity. The time line will help us determine who had the opportunity. In other words, do they have a legitimate alibi as to where they were at the time of the murder? But first, we must determine the time of the murder. Motive will be revealed via the interviews."

The chief then again addressed Dani, "Were you able to lift any usable finger prints from the doors, windows, or patio furniture?"

"Yes," Dani replied. "A couple of small ones which were probably the kids. But also a few larger ones."

The chief instructed, "Contact the FBI and run those prints through IAFIS and see if we get a hit. Start it immediately. With over 70 million prints on file, I'm not sure what their turnaround time is."

Finally, the chief explained, "I'm going to spend some time with Mr. Steve Winter. Witnesses saw and heard his motorcycle on the street this morning. A no show for work when he was supposed to be there on that very same street at the exact spot that morning - far too coincidental. His name shouts opportunity. This doesn't leave this room, but right now Steve is our primary suspect. He has a lot of explaining to do."

Aaron addressed the chief, this time using his first name, "Fred, do you really think Steve is capable of committing murder? If so, why Stacy?"

The chief responded, "If you don't already know this, you will quickly learn that it is shocking who is capable of committing murder. More than you would care to imagine. As for the why, don't forget that Steve and Stacy dated before she met Shane. After the divorce, Steve had tried to re-connect with her. But that went nowhere. I'm not saying he did it. Right now, all we have are suspects. I'll tell the press we have one or two persons of interest. That's all Mike and others in the press need to know for now. Do your job, work the case. We'll see if other suspects come up, but for now, let's work what is right in front of us."

"One last question, Boss." this time it was Eric. "What about a transient. There's a few homeless squatters outside of town. Any chance one of them could have wandered in and killed her?"

The chief explained, "Possible, yes. But not probable. They have no motive to just murder someone. There is no evidence of the house being broken into. Nothing appears to be stolen. We didn't see any bruises or any other signs of a struggle on her body. She was fully clothed, so sexual molestation isn't likely. We'll wait for the coroner's report. Unless there is something in the report or some other evidence turns up, it's highly unlikely to have been a transient. I have far greater concerns with the people we've discussed. Let's deal with what we've got right in front of us and see where we go from there."

All three officers nodded and Aaron spoke, "We're on it sir."

Just then, Michelle walked into the room and said, "Chief, the coroner's office just called. They said that Dr. Terrace would have his preliminary report early afternoon tomorrow."

"Good enough. Thanks Michelle. Now, lets all get to work," the chief concluded.

"One more thing," Michelle added. "Mike Lambeau is in the office, waiting to see you."

As they all walked out of the conference room, the chief told Michelle to show Mike into his office.

When Chief Earl took over as the Chief of Police, he did not move into his predecessor's large office. Instead, he had that office converted into a conference room. He stayed in the smaller, corner office where he had been working for three years as the assistant to the chief. He had a large, dark brown mahogany desk with a matching credenza behind the desk. Two photos were on his credenza. One was of his wife, whom he had married shortly after being discharged from the army. Next to that was a photo of him and his buddy, Fire Chief Gary Patrick, holding a stringer of trout from one of their many fishing trips. His leather desk chair had a high back and arm rests. Two chairs sat at the front of the desk. He figured if there were more than two people who needed to see him, they would simply meet in the conference room.

The walls had dark wood paneling three feet up from the floor. The rest of the walls were painted a dark, forest green. On one wall, he had a large framed copy of the United States Declaration of Independence. Above that was a U.S. flag in a triangular display case. It was the flag presented to his mother when his father had passed away, at the age of seventy-two. "From a grateful nation," the honor guard had said as they handed her the flag, graveside. His father had served in the army and had seen action in the Pacific at the very end of World War Two.

To the left of the Declaration of Independence, he had three Civil War photos. One was a copy of an old photo from Gettysburg, a view of the sloping field of Pickette's charge. The second was a copy of an old photo of Abraham Lincoln standing next to General Ulysses S. Grant, standing near a tent at General Grant's camp headquarters. The third was a copy of an artist's rendering of General Lee's surrender to General Grant at Appomattox, Virginia. To the left of the three framed Civil War photos were two framed copies of President Lincoln documents. One; a copy of the entire Gettysburg's Address. The other; a duplication of the opening comments of the Emancipation Proclamation.

To the right of the Declaration of Independence, he had three World War Two photos. One was a copy of the photo of the flag being raised on Iwo Jima. The second was a copy of the photo of Japan's formal surrender, the official surrender documents signed on board the battleship U.S.S. Missouri. The surrender photo is of Fleet Admiral Chester W. Nimitz, singing the Instrument of Surrender as the U.S. Representative. General Douglas MacArthur, standing behind him. The bottom photo was of a B-17 Flying Fortress Bomber, ready for takeoff. To the right of those photos was a framed copy of President Franklin D. Roosevelt's Pearl Harbor address to the nation.

In that corner of the office, Chief Earl had an American flag on a pole in a stand. At the top of the flagpole was a gold plated eagle. It would be an understatement to say that Chief Earl was unashamedly patriotic.

Chief Earl returned to his office and Michelle showed Mike Lambeau into his office. Mike immediately began, "Chief Earl, I know how busy you are, but what can you tell me about the Stacy Pruitt murder case?"

"Whoa, Mike. Who told you she was murdered?" the chief demanded.

"It's all over town, Chief. Are you saying she wasn't murdered?" Mike asked.

The chief replied, "All I'm saying is that we are waiting for the coroner's report to determine the cause of death and then we can begin to figure out if she was in fact, murdered."

"Fair enough," Mike said, "So officially, the cause of death is to be determined pending the report of the coroner. Any idea when that will happen?"

"Tomorrow afternoon, we hope," was the quick answer.

Mike continued, "Can you answer some of the questions you couldn't answer this morning? Such as, were there any other bodies found?"

"There were no other bodies found," another quick answer.

Mike said, "Were there any weapons found."

"Can't give out that information while the investigation is ongoing" the chief said, solemnly.

Frustrated, Mike said, "Can you at least tell me where the body was found. The word on the street is that it was found on the back porch."

The chief's eyes brightened, "Yes, I can tell you that. She was found on the back porch."

Mike wrote in his notebook, and then asked, "Do you know who was the last one to see her alive or when she was last seen alive?"

The chief responded, "We do not have that information as of yet, but if we did, that information could not be discussed during the investigation."

"What about fingerprints or DNA stuff?" Mike asked.

"We have a few prints. Probably from Stacy and the kids, but we're going to run them all through IAFIS just to be sure," the chief answered.

"I'm sorry, what is IAFIS?" Mike asked.

"Integrated Automated Fingerprint Identification System. It's an international database of fingerprints managed by the FBI," the chief explained.

"When will that be done?" Mike questioned.

"We'll submit them today, but one never knows what the response time is. It depends on how many requests they are receiving at that moment. Thousands of police agencies from across the U.S., in fact, from around the world, have access. Requests are prioritized to a certain degree: criminal verses civil, for example. So, depending on the volume of current request, it could be a couple of hours or it could be a couple of days."

Mike scribbled some notes in his book, then continued, "Is it true that Josh Allen found the body?"

The chief hesitated.

Mike pleaded, "Come on chief. I saw him sitting on the front porch this morning. I talked to him when he got ready to leave."

The chief nodded, "Yes, Josh found her. But I can give no details as to why, how or when."

Mike pushed, "Come on Chief, can you give me something?"

"Something? Here's something. Stacy Pruitt was found dead this morning on her back porch. The cause of death has yet to be determined. No other bodies were found. The coroner hopes to have his preliminary report by tomorrow afternoon. Fingerprints have been submitted to IAFIS. Officers are working the case. I'd say that's a pretty big 'something.'"

Mike said, "Please Chief Earl, I'm just trying to do my job."

Growing impatient, the chief retorted, "And I'm just trying to do my job. Which I can't do as long as I'm having to help you do your job."

Mike looked at the chief for a minute, then closed his notebook, got up and started to the door.

The chief said, "Hey, Mike. Look, we're in a tough spot here. As soon as I get the coroner's report tomorrow, I'll be able to give you some more info. But right now, I've given you as much as I can."

Mike nodded and then said, "I understand. I don't mean to be a pain or anything. We've both got to do what we've got to do. I'll talk to you tomorrow. And, oh, by the way, the TV station from up north is sending a news crew down. Heads up!"

To which the chief replied, "Great. Just what I need. But, thanks for the warning."

The next morning, each of the officers set up appointments for their interviews.
Chief Earl, however, went straight to Steve Winter's home early that morning. Steve's house had recently received a fresh coat of paint. Something he and Josh had done when they had a couple of days between jobs. The front yard had patches of grass, but not enough to cover all of the dirt. With just a little bit of care and attention, the grass might have a fighting chance of covering the entire yard. A few leaves were scattered across the yard, the first of

many leaves which would fall as the weather continued to get cooler. The flower boxes sat empty for lack of anyone taking the time to plant flowers.

When Steve opened his garage door and was about to get onto his motorcycle to head to work, he was surprised to see the police car in his driveway, the chief standing there, leaning against the front left fender. The chief had on a long brown overcoat to protect him from the coolness of the morning. The chief said, "Morning Steve."

Steve, looking startled, said, "Hi. Didn't expect to see you here. What's up Chief Earl?" He was wearing a leather jacket and was just about to put on a pair of leather gloves. Instead, he set the gloves on the seat of his motorcycle, next to his helmet.

"I've got a few questions for you regarding Stacy Pruitt," the chief explained.

Steve answered, "Oh. Well, okay. But I wasn't there when Josh found her. Don't know that I can be much help."

"For starters, when was the last time you saw Stacy?" the chief asked.

Steve replied, "Oh, I don't know, maybe a week or so."

"A week or so? Are you sure you haven't seen her since then?" the chief continued.

"Yep. Pretty much sure. About a week or so," Steve said again.

The chief pursued, "You didn't see her yesterday morning, real early? Or maybe late the night before?"

"No sir. I'd certainly remember that," Steve insisted.

The chief changed the question, "Okay Steve. Why didn't you go to work yesterday?"

"Well, I did go to work. I was just a little bit late," Steve said.

"How little?" the chief pressed.

"About two hours," Steve clarified.

"That's an awfully big little. Would you mind telling me why you were late?" the chief asked.

"I overslept. Just one of those things. Hey, wait a minute. Are you and Josh pranking me for being late yesterday? Did he put you up to this? Boy, that's a good one. You got me!" Steve said laughing.

The chief did not smile, he simply said, "No, we aren't pranking you. This isn't a joke. Tell me again why you were two hours late?"

Steve shuffled his feet, feeling like a kid who was just sent to the principal's office, "I overslept. It's as simple as that."

"You were sleeping the whole time?" the chief asked again.

"Yes," Steve replied.

"Were you out earlier in the morning?" the chief pressed.

"No, asleep in bed. No witnesses though, just me and my blanket," Steve said with a slight grin.

"You see, Steve, that's the problem. There are witnesses. You were seen riding your motorcycle on Stacy's street early yesterday morning," the chief said very pointedly.

Steve looked at the ground. Then he replied, "I'm not the only one who owns a motorcycle in this town. Could have been anyone."

The chief then said, "How many Harley's do you suppose there are in our little town? And how many of those Harley owners know where Stacy lives and would just coincidently be riding up her street early the very same morning of her death? And how many of those Harley owners have a history with Stacy? Do you suppose any of them used to date her?"

Then he added, "Steve, let me ask you again. Were you riding your motorcycle on Elm Street early yesterday morning?"

After a long pause, Steve murmured, "Yes, sir. I was."

"Can you tell me why you were there?" the chief continued.

Again, a long awkward pause. Then Steve shook his head and said, "No. I can't tell you why. It's a private matter."

The chief then quietly said, "A private matter? Then, Steve, I'm going to have to take you down to the station for a few more questions."

Steve's head jerked up from looking at the ground, "Are you arresting me!?"

The chief replied, "No, not at this time. I'm just bringing you in for some further questions."

"But, I'm supposed to be at work," Steve pleaded.

"Looks like you're going to be just a little bit late," the chief explained. "I'll have Michelle call Josh once we get to the station."

Steve closed the garage door and walked over to the chief's patrol car. The chief put him in the back seat and they drove down to the station.

The chief put Steve in one of the cells and said, "Care to let me know now why you were driving your motorcycle on Elm Street early yesterday morning and why you lied about the reason you were late to work?"

Steve gloomily replied, "Chief Earl, I just can't tell you. As I said, it's a private matter."

"Steve, I want to make sure you understand the magnitude of the situation you are in. Right now, you are here for questioning and you have refused to answer a very critical question. I hope you realize what impression that gives. I can only hold you so long for questioning. At some point in time, I will have to consider charges. So, your 'private matter' is developing into something that can have enormous consequences. Are you understanding all of this?" the chief demanded.

"Yes, sir. I just can't say anything right now," Steve said sadly.

"Not right now? Well then, let's let you think about all of this for a while," the chief said sternly.

He then turned and walked into his office.

Chapter Nine: Questions

Officer Dani began her day with a visit to Dr. Clevenger. Seventy-one year old Dr. Don Clevenger had been retired for six years. Skinny as a rail with a large hooked nose, he enjoyed walking the neighborhood and spending time in his gardens. He also enjoyed reading mystery novels while sipping on a cup of tea or a nice glass of red wine. He was exactly six feet tall, but his slender build made him look a bit taller. His thinning gray hair was often covered with a stylish Panama hat. He wore the hat to protect his head from the sun as much as for the classic style. He was what some would call an old-school gentleman: prim, proper and courteous. He was highly respected in the community. Widowed for three years, the thought of dating had never crossed his mind. Conversely, dating him had crossed the minds of many Springerville widows.

Dani knocked on his door and was greeted very warmly by a man who looked dapper. He managed to look very casual while simultaneously looking classy. Dr. Clevenger said, "Well, good morning young lady. What can I do for you today?"

Before she could answer, they were interrupted by the barking of Dr. Clevenger's dog, Baxter, a friendly and energetic Springer Spaniel. Dani quickly bent over and put her hands on both sides of the dog's head and started scratching behind his ears. The dog wagged his tail which shook his entire chocolate brown and white patched body. The doctor smiled and said, "You've just made a friend for life! I can put him out back if he gets to be a nuisance."

Dani smiled and said, "Not at all. I love dogs, especially cute little guys like this!" She then stood and said, "Good morning Dr. Clevenger. My name is Dani and I'm with the police department. Do you mind if I come in and ask you a few questions?"

"I would enjoy the company. Please come in. May I get you some coffee or tea or even a glass of water?" Clevenger enthused.

"Oh no. But thank you very much," Dani replied.

"No problem at all. I just returned from taking Baxter for a walk. We love our morning walks," the doctor explained.

They entered into the front room and sat on a matching set of arm chairs, with a small table between them. On the table was the morning paper and a pair of reading glasses, plus a cup of hot tea. Baxter immediately laid down next to the doctor's chair.

Dani said, "You mentioned how much you enjoy your morning walks. In fact, that's why I'm here. Were you walking over on Elm Street early yesterday morning?"

The doctor said, "Yes, I was walking Baxter. Weather permitting, that's our morning ritual."

Dani asked, "Did you go by Stacy Pruitt's house?"

"Yes, I suppose I did. I heard the tragic news. What a terrible thing to happen in our peaceful little town," Clevenger answered.

"Did you stop at her house for any reason?" Dani continued.

Surprised, the doctor said, "No, why would I stop there?"

Dani smiled and said, "Just checking. Did you see anyone else at or near her house?"

"No," he said.

"Did you see anyone else out walking or jogging or driving by?" Dani asked.

"I had a short conversation with the widow Perkins. In fact, she's the reason I was walking on Elm," said the doctor.

Dani asked, "How so?"

Dr. Clevenger explained, "I usually walk around my block. But Anne Perkins would stop me every morning and talk my leg off. I didn't want to be rude, so I'd listen and nod my head as if I were interested in what she was saying. I just wanted to finish my morning walk, get a little walk in for my dog, and then get back home to my paper and breakfast. I decided to try a different route yesterday morning just to see if I could avoid her. Darned if she didn't drive up, pull over, roll down her window and start jabbering away."

Dani continued with her questions, "Do you remember what time you had that conversation with Mrs. Perkins?"

"Well, let's see, I leave my house at seven o'clock. I'd say it was about fifteen minutes later. So, seven-fifteen or so," Dr. Clevenger answered.

Dani asked, "Did you see anyone else walking or jogging or driving by on Elm yesterday morning, other than Mrs. Perkins?"

Dr. Clevenger pondered the question, then said, "No. Nothing out of the ordinary. Can't remember if any cars passed by. Couldn't honestly say one way or the other. But I don't recall seeing anything else."

"Did you happen to see a motorcycle?" Dani asked.

Both eyes widened a bit as Clevenger said, "Well, by golly, I did indeed see a motorcycle. I'm sorry, I plum forgot about that."

"Was that while you were talking to Mrs. Perkins?" Dani continued.

"Well, let me think. No, that was before I saw her. I was about half way up the street, when it drove by. It turned right at the corner. Anne came around the corner shortly after the bike passed," Clevenger recalled.

"Would you, by any chance, happen to know what kind of motorcycle it was?" Dani asked.

"I'm pretty sure it was a Harley. They have a very distinct sound you know. A soft rumble, as it were," Clevenger explained.

"Is there anything else you can think of that might be pertinent to our investigation?" Dani smiled as she asked this last question.

"No. Don't think so. It's a terrible shame though. A terrible shame. Stacy was always such a sweet girl. But in these past few years she had changed so much. It's like she wasn't the same person. She seemed so sad, so lonely, so frustrated with life. It's like she had been living a life of misery. Who knows, maybe it's a blessing that her suffering is over."

Dani pondered his last statement, then politely said, "Thank you for your time Dr. Clevenger."

She then stood and Dr. Clevenger showed her to the door.

From there, Dani drove halfway around the block to the home of Anne Perkins. Anne was sitting on her front porch, in her rocking chair. There was a small covey of birds in her front yard, waiting for the bread that Anne was slowly breaking into small pieces and throwing onto the lawn. The birds would flutter back and forth from the branches of an Elm tree down to the yard as they snatched up the small bits of bread.

As Dani walked up the front walkway to the porch, the birds scattered. Dani said, "Good morning Mrs. Perkins. Do you mind if I sit and visit with you for a minute or two?"

"I would love the company, how nice of you, please have a seat," Mrs. Perkins gushed. Then, seeing Dani's uniform she said, "Oh dear. Is this about my little accident yesterday, that little meeting I had with the fire hydrant? I'm so sorry. Do you have to take me to jail now?"

As she took a seat on a porch swing next to Anne's rocking chair, Dani quickly replied, "No, no, no. This is not about that at all. That's all been taken care of. The new fire hydrant has already been installed. And you are not ever going to jail for that. My name is Dani, and as you have already figured out, I work for the police department. I just have a question about something else."

Relieved, Anne smiled and then said, "Oh, good. I was so worried. I feel so bad about that. But please, how can I help you my dear?"

Dani smiled at her and then asked, "Yesterday morning, as you were driving to Truman's, did you happen to see Dr. Clevenger while he was walking his dog?"

With a very large grin, Mrs. Perkins enthusiastically replied, "Yes, I saw Dr. Clevenger. He's such a nice man. Handsome, too! He's a friend of mine. We stop and talk whenever we see each other on the street. Yes, I saw him yesterday morning, before I went to the market. Why do you ask? Is he okay?"

Dani again quickly responded, "Absolutely. I just came from his house. He's fine and so is his dog, Baxter. But let me ask, when you were visiting with Dr. Clevenger, did you see or hear anything else?"

Mrs. Perkins, looking confused, asked, "What do you mean? Was I supposed to be looking for something?"

Dani explained, "No ma'am. I mean, did you see anyone else walking that morning. Or see any cars drive by while you were talking to Dr. Clevenger?"

Mrs. Perkins said, "Well, um, no, just that one motorcycle that went by right before I turned onto the street where I met the doctor."

"A motorcycle?" Dani quizzed.

Mrs. Perkins replied, "Yes. It's one of those, oh, what do they call them, a Marley."

Trying not to laugh, Dani asked, "Do you mean a Harley?"

"Yes! That's what they call them, a Harley. They're very loud." Mrs. Perkins stated.

"Yes, they are. Do you know who was riding it?" asked Dani.

Mrs. Perkins answered, "No, couldn't tell. They go very fast."

"Yes, they do. What direction was the motorcycle going?" Dani continued.

"It had come up the same street Dr. Clevenger was on. Then it turned onto the street where I was driving. I was going one way, it was going the other. That's all I remember," Mrs. Perkins explained.

Dani then said, "One last question: do you remember what time you and Dr. Clevenger were on Elm?"

Mrs. Perkins thought for a moment and then said, "It must have been ten or fifteen minutes after seven o'clock."

Standing, Dani said, "Thank you Mrs. Perkins."

"Officer," Mrs. Perkins continued, "May I ask you one quick question please?"

"Certainly," Dani responded.

"Why would such a beautiful little girl become a police officer?" Mrs. Perkins asked.

Dani smiled politely and said, "I just want to help good people. Good people like you, Mrs. Perkins."

Mrs. Perkins beamed and said, "Well, I think that is wonderful. Thank you for being my police officer!"

Now, it was Dani's turn to grin. She bent down and gave Mrs. Perkins a hug and said, "It is my pleasure to be your police officer. You have a nice day. And thank you for your help."

With that, Dani walked out to her patrol car. As she approached her car, she noticed a vehicle slowly driving up the street. As it passed her, she saw that it was being driven by Mike Lambeau. Since he was coming from the direction of Elm Street, she assumed he was getting a few pictures of the crime scene or, perhaps, interviewing neighbors for a story. She then got into her patrol car and returned to the station.

Chief Earl called Michelle into his office and asked her to call Josh Allen to inform him that Steve would not be in to work today because he was being held for questioning at the station. As she turned to leave, the chief changed his mind and said, "On second thought, I'll make that call myself. Please track down his phone number and bring it here to me."

A minute or two later, Michelle brought the phone number into the chief. He thanked her and dialed Josh's number and informed him that he had Steve Winter sitting in a cell at the police station, and therefore, Steve would be late for work, at best. Of course, Josh was shocked and asked why in the world the chief would arrest Steve.

The chief replied, "He's not arrested. I brought him in to ask a few questions."

Josh simply stated, "Sounds like he's been arrested to me."

The chief reassured him, "No, he has not been arrested, just detained. He will be detained until he answers a few questions. In fact, I have a question for you. Did Steve ever show up for work yesterday?"

Josh informed him that yes, Steve had indeed shown up for work.

The chief then said, "Well, how late was he? We were there for some time!"

Josh said, "He was a little over two hours late."

"Did he say why?" the chief asked.

"Sure. Said he overslept," Josh answered.

"Overslept - two hours," the chief said, "Josh, I've got a few more questions for you about Steve. Would you mind coming down to the station so we can talk? It'd be a lot easier than on the phone, if you can get away from your job site."

Josh responded, "The quickest I can get there would be right after lunch. I've just poured some concrete for a small patio and I can't walk away right at the moment. Especially without Steve here to help me work it."

"That'll work. I appreciate it, Josh. I'll see you then," the chief thanked Josh and hung up his phone.

Meanwhile, Officer Aaron had the task of meeting with Coach Stewart. He had called the school that morning to schedule an appointment with the coach. The coach was able to get someone to cover his second hour P.E. class and agreed to meet Aaron in the coach's office. Aaron had also called Richard White to set up a meeting. Richard said he was busy all morning but could meet him over lunch.

Aaron walked into the coach's office as scheduled. The coach spoke first, "You've come a long way since playing for me back in the day."

Aaron smiled and said, "Those were the good ol' days, for sure. Lots of great memories." Aaron then spotted the Spirit Spear standing in the corner of the coach's office, "Wow, that brings back memories."

"That spear has inspired many a defense. 'Who's going to be the point of the spear?' I'd yell. You guys would run onto the field like a bunch of crazed mad men!" the coach smiled as he reminisced.

"The point of the spear" resonated in Aaron's mind. He walked over to take a closer look at the spear, as if admiring it. The roughly hewn metal tip of the spear looked just like it did those many years ago.

As Aaron focused upon the point of the spear, Coach Stewart said, "You were what, two years or so ahead of Shane?"

"Yes," Aaron said as he turned his attention back to the coach, "Exactly two years. I graduated before his glory days. But I did get to see him play a couple of times. I was away at the police academy at that time. But the few times I saw him play, he was impressive. Heck of a player. Good guy, too."

"One of the best," Coach continued, "Going to be an outstanding head coach someday. Great potential. Who knows, maybe coach college someday, if other things in his life don't get in his way."

"What kind of 'other things' do you mean, Coach?" Aaron pursued.

"You know, he's had a string of bad luck. Gets his knee blown out. Then that girl gets pregnant and he has to get married, as if she didn't know exactly what she was doing. No big surprise when that ends in divorce. Loses everything in his divorce, but still has two kids he's responsible for. Now his ex goes and gets herself murdered. Another thing he's got to deal with. Gotta raise two kids who don't even have a mama any more. One big setback after another. If he could just catch a break..."

The coach was silent for a minute, so Aaron said, "Coach, would you say that Shane was your favorite player here of all time?"

The coach looked at Aaron and said, "We aren't supposed to have favorites. We certainly aren't supposed to show any favoritism. People can't handle that, especially parents. But just between you, me and the doorpost, Shane was like a son to me. Now, I know he's got a dad and he's a real good man. He and Shane have a great relationship. But I was his coach. He's the most naturally talented player we've ever had here. He's got a head for football, knows the game in and out. Understood it early, which is part of the reason he excelled. So, honestly, yes, he's special to me and always will be. It pains me to see what happened to him. And that girl has turned out to be nothing but trouble for him."

Aaron let the words sink in, and then said, "You know Coach. I like Shane, too. Most everyone does. But he's not perfect. In Stacy's defense, no one forced Shane to move in with her in college. He's a stand-up guy and chose to take the high road in getting married. Obviously, their marriage wasn't perfect, but Shane is just as much to blame as Stacy. You make it seem that she wrecked his life. Far from it. They had their challenges like a lot of young couples do, both made mistakes, and sadly, they didn't work it out. Her death is a tragedy! Recently, he's had a hard life, but hers is over!"

The coach was not happy with Aaron's assessment. He glared at Aaron and bluntly stated, "Look kid. You see what is. I see what can be. I see potential. That's what good coaches do. And I'm telling you, Shane has potential! And that girl has proven over and over that she was the biggest obstacle to him reaching that potential."

Aaron shook his head and said simply, "I think you're wrong, Coach."

The coach stood up and said, "Do you want to know what I think? I'll tell you what I think! The best thing to happen to Shane is to finally have that girl out of his life! That's what I think."

Aaron looked up at the coach and asked, "Coach, where were you yesterday morning, early?"

The coach looked bewildered, and then, stunned. He stood speechless, then slowly sat down. Through gritted teeth he said, "Are you suggesting that I had anything to do with that girl's death?"

Aaron, refusing to temper his comments even a little, said, "That girl had a name. Her name was Stacy. She was murdered yesterday morning. I asked you a question: Where were you yesterday morning?"

The coach, now seething, said, "Who the hell do you think you are, coming into my office and insinuating such a thing? You can take your question and shove it. Get out!"

Aaron, very calmly but pointedly, said, "Coach, I'm no longer one of your players. I'm an officer with the police department. I am here investigating a crime. I have not accused you of anything. I am merely gathering information about the crime. I have asked you one simple question and I will repeat it for the third time. If you refuse to answer the question, I will have no choice but to take you down to the station to be questioned by Chief Earl. Again, where were you yesterday morning, early?"

The two sat, staring at each other. Neither giving an inch. Aaron had no idea what to expect next, but he knew it would not be a long conversation, if any conversation at all. The silence continued.

Finally, the coach began to look around the room. Staring at wall plaques, trophies, boxes, a few water bottles, a stack of orange cones, a chalk board with a few diagrams of football plays drawn on it, a large bag stuffed with footballs, a stack of jerseys, a clipboard hanging from a nail and the Spirit Spear standing in the corner. The coach continued to stare at the Spirit Spear as Aaron patiently waited. Then, the coach spoke, "So, it's come down to this. Well, I'll tell you where I was. I was sitting right here, doing my job. I had a coaches meeting at six-thirty. That's the answer to your question, asked three times, 'where was I?' Right here. I wouldn't want to get within ten yards of that girl."

Aaron noticed that as the coach spoke, his breathing became a little more intense, his eyes were squinted as he glared at Aaron and a large vein on the side of his neck began to bulge.

Aaron's disgust for the coach's attitude toward Stacy was palpable and it was causing his own blood to boil. He could feel the hair on the back of his neck rise. He realized that both he and the coach were in danger of letting their anger get the best of them. But he knew he had to ask a few more questions, beginning with the question as to whether there were any witnesses who could confirm that he was in his office. He anticipated another explosive, confrontational response from the coach. But it never happened.

Before he could ask the question, the school bell rang. The coach looked at the clock and stood to leave. As he did so he said, "I've got a class to get to. We're done here."

Aaron quickly said, "Just a few more questions, coach."

The coach glared at Aaron and said, "I'm done. You'll have to come back if you insist on asking any more of your stupid questions."

"I'll drop by after school today," Aaron said.

The coach responded as he walked toward the door, "Nope. Got football practice right after school. Try again tomorrow, if you must." With that, the coach walked out the door.

Aaron sat for a moment and then realized that he had balled both his hands into fists. He slowly opened his hands, looked around the office, took one last look at the Spirit Spear, and then went out to his patrol car and headed back to the office.

Dani had made her way back to the station and found the chief. She was surprised to see Steve Winter sitting in one of the holding cells. She gave her report to the chief concerning her interviews with Dr. Clevenger and Anne

Perkins. She also mentioned seeing Mike Lambeau driving in the neighborhood.

The chief listened carefully and then said, "Good job. Write it all up. Every detail. Then see if Eric needs any help. Thanks."

Dani returned to her desk and began to write up her report. She had just gotten started when a delivery man entered the office carrying a bouquet of flowers. She and Eric looked at each other, somewhat surprised, as the delivery man approached Dani's desk.

"Are you Michelle?" he asked.

Before Dani could answer, Michelle smiled and said, "That would be me."

The delivery man walked over to Michelle's desk and placed the flowers on her desk. Michelle handed him a small tip and thanked him. Still smiling, she read the card and then moved some of the flowers around as she straightened up the arrangement.

Eric immediately got up and walked over to Michelle's desk and asked, "Who are these from?"

Michelle looked at him for a few seconds and then said, "They are from a friend."

Eric responded, "Well, I didn't think they were from a stranger! If he's sending you flowers, he's more than a friend. Come on, out with it girl, spill the beans, who sent you flowers?"

Michelle placed the card into her purse and snapped it shut. She then looked at Eric and said, "This falls into the category of None-Of-Your-Business." She then returned to her work.

Eric thought for a minute and said, "Remember, I am actually very good at detective work. It shouldn't take me much time to track down who this secret admirer is."

Without looking up from her work, Michelle replied, "You need to remember that I am the one who calculates your hours and fills out your paycheck before the chief signs it. It wouldn't take me long to forget about some of your overtime hours. Furthermore, this 'secret admirer' is no secret to me. And, it's still none of your business."

Eric started to respond, but then thought better of it. He simply shook his head, laughed, and returned to his desk.

Dani then said to Michelle, "Way to go Michelle! It's none of Mr. Nosey's business. This is just something that will stay between us girls. You can tell me later, when it's just the two of us."

Michelle smiled, sighed and said, "Nice try Dani. But no. It's no more your business than it is his. In this office what's my business is only my business and it will stay my business. Anyone who crosses that line will pay the consequences."

Eric quickly jumped in, "And what are the consequences?"

Michelle looked up from her work and stared at Eric.

Eric quickly said, "Never mind."

Dani started laughing and said, "Smooth, officer, very smooth."

To which Eric replied, "Yeah, like you did so much better with your 'just us girls' gender thing."

Dani wadded up a piece of paper and threw it across the room at Eric. He caught the ball of paper and threw it back at Dani, and said, "Now you're messing with the superior gender!"

Dani quickly retorted, "Obviously you meant the delusional gender."

Michelle just shook her head. Neither of the other two noticed the very slight smile she managed to keep hidden from them as she continued her work, occasionally glancing at the beautiful arrangement of flowers.

Chapter Ten: Guilty, But Innocent?

As it approached noon, Aaron made his way over to Lisa's Kitchen, a favorite café for the Main Street professionals to gather for lunch. The breakfast menu included the usual assortment of pancakes, waffles, eggs, sausage, bacon, biscuits and gravy, muffins, yogurt, oatmeal, hash browns, seasonal fruit, and a few more items. The lunch menu had traditional American cuisine: soups, salads, potato skins, onion rings, chili, various sandwiches, wraps, burgers, fries, etc. A limited dessert menu included homemade cookies, fudge, pies, shakes and ice cream. The tables were decorated with red and white checkered tablecloths and red napkins. Each table had a small arrangement of fresh cut flowers as a center piece, most often harvested from Lisa's own flower gardens. The café, open Monday through Friday, closed each day at 3:00 and was not open for dinner. Lisa believed strongly that evenings and weekends were for family.

Richard had found a corner booth at the café where he and Aaron could speak privately. As Aaron entered, he saw Richard waving him over to the booth. Aaron sat down and the waitress came over with two menus. Aaron hesitated. He hadn't planned on eating while doing business, but he did need to have lunch and he wasn't sure how long this would take. Besides, perhaps Richard would let down his guard just a bit if they were breaking bread together. That is, if he had any reason to keep his guard up in the first place. Both Aaron and Richard thanked the waitress. She then took their drink orders, diet soda for Aaron, ice tea for Richard, and then she left the table.

Richard then said, "This one's on me." Aaron quickly replied, "Now wait a minute, I asked you to meet. This is business so it should be on me."

"Nonsense," Richard said, "All of our businesses rely on and appreciate your tremendous service to our community.

The least we can do is pick up the tab for lunch once in a while. I insist."

Aaron, quickly started running through his head the question of ethical compromise if an officer accepts lunch from a potential murder suspect. He also knew that the chief frowned upon any of his officers receiving free meals, or even discounts, because they were an officer, especially while on duty. But Aaron thought that this was a unique situation and that there are always exceptions to every rule, so he decided that the smart action would be to allow Richard to buy, or at least to let Richard think he was buying. So, he smiled and said, "Thanks."

The waitress returned and Richard ordered a Cob Salad, vinaigrette dressing on the side. Aaron ordered a BLT sandwich with sweet potato fries.

Richard then said, "Well, why not let's get right to the point of the discussion? I'm still numb. Maybe I'm in shock, I don't know. It's very surreal. I can't believe Stacy is dead. Please tell me, how is the investigation going?"

Aaron replied, "Well Richard, you know how thorough and meticulous Chief Earl is. He will leave no stone unturned."

"Good!" Richard responded, "That's one of the reasons he has such an excellent reputation in this town. He gets the job done and done right!"

"You'll get no argument from me concerning the chief. He does indeed do the job the way it's supposed to be done. Along that line, I need to ask you a question," Aaron stated.

"Sure. I guess that's why we're here. Go ahead," Richard said.

Aaron explained, "Yesterday you told the chief the last time you saw Stacy was at lunch the day before."

"Yes, I did," Richard said slowly.

"But in fact, we have witnesses who saw you two at dinner the night before," Aaron added.

Richard looked down at his hands. Before he could respond, Aaron added, "Furthermore, the witnesses allege that the two of you got into a heated argument. A very heated argument. Is this true?"

Richard slowly nodded and mumbled, "Yes, it's true."

"Of course, you can see why the chief is concerned about this?" Aaron stated.

"Yeah, I guess so," Richard confessed.

"You guess so?!" Aaron said, incredulously. "Richard, let me spell it out for you. I'm not sure if you are seeing the full magnitude of what we're talking about. First, the lady you've been dating for about two years is murdered. That same day, you lie to Chief Earl, the CHIEF, about having dinner with her the night before. Then, later, we find out that you not only had dinner with her, but that you had an intense argument with her, to the point that she stormed out of the restaurant, which could not have made you very happy. Then, the very day after her murder, you show up to work as if nothing happened. You don't close your office for the day, you don't stay home and grieve, it's just business as usual. Who does that? Please tell me you understand how this looks and why the chief wanted me to talk to you today."

Richard slid back in his seat and began wringing the napkin in his hands. He nodded a few times but didn't immediately speak. Aaron waited. Finally, fighting back tears, Richard explained, very quietly, "As far as working today: I would go stark raving mad if I sat by myself in an empty apartment. Stacy's parents don't like me. They tolerate me, but they don't like me. Her kids can't stand me. Honestly, I don't know why. My best guess is that I'm not their dad, I'm not Shane. But the point is, I certainly can't go to her parents' house today. I have no family here in Springerville. For my own sanity, I had to get out of the apartment and do something. I decided I would just work. I had appointments all morning anyway. It wasn't easy. They all wanted to extend their condolences and talk about Stacy. I just felt that working was much better than sitting at home in misery. At least I wasn't alone. That's why I asked if we could meet over lunch; I just don't want to be alone."

Aaron listened patiently, then said, "Okay, I'll buy all that. But why lie to the chief about dinner? What difference did it make if you had lunch with her or dinner with her?"

"The difference was the argument," Richard responded. "I envy guys like Chief Earl and Doc Clevenger and Chief Patrick and Pastor Bergeson and others. They are all highly respected. I would like to earn that respect, too. Some of the business men and women in town have it, some don't. I think it has to be earned. It isn't automatic, regardless of your title or your job. So, when Stacy had her meltdown and stormed out of the restaurant, I was humiliated. That doesn't help build credibility and trust. That's fodder for the gossips of the community. I certainly didn't want to talk about it or have to relive it. And, I was numb after the chief dropped that bombshell on me. Can you even begin to imagine my state of mind? I was hardly thinking at all, let alone thinking clearly. So, yes, I lied to the chief about having dinner with Stacy. I wish that I hadn't. But I did. And I will personally apologize to him for being so stupid."

At that moment, the waitress brought their food. She said, cheerily, "Here you go guys, can I get you anything else?"

Aaron quickly said, "No thank you. We're good." She looked at Richard for his response, but he continued to stare at the table. She looked back at Aaron and then quickly walked away.

"I'm sorry you're having to go through this. I'm sorry you lost Stacy. I'm sorry you're hurting. And, I'm very sorry I've had to have this conversation with you. But I appreciate your candor," Aaron said. Then he continued, "Having said all of that, I do need to ask you a few more questions. I need more details."

Richard nodded.

Aaron continued, "Would you mind telling me what you and Stacy were arguing about? I imagine it is a personal matter, but in light of the situation, the question has to be asked. But please understand, this will be kept confidential."

With a gloomy expression, Richard responded, "I understand. I asked about us moving in together and she said no, again. We've had this discussion a couple of times before with the same result. So, this time I pushed a little, trying to persuade her. I guess I pushed a little too hard because she went ballistic. She raised her voice and I tried to calm her down. She then stood and shouted something about me always trying to control her and then turned and stormed out. I was shocked. And humiliated. It was very embarrassing, to say the least."

"I'm sorry to hear that," Aaron replied, "That had to be very awkward for you."

"Ha! Awkward doesn't begin to express how foolish I felt," Richard explained.

Aaron continued, "Do you have any idea where Stacy went after she left you sitting in the restaurant?"

"I have no idea," Richard replied. "I would guess she went home. Or maybe over to Dotty's house. They spend a lot of time together. When Stacy's upset, she oftentimes ends up at Dotty's."

"But, she didn't say where she was going? And you haven't heard from anyone else as to where she might have gone other than home that evening?" Aaron asked.

"The last time I saw her was at the restaurant. When she stormed out, she certainly didn't bother to tell me where she was going," Richard explained.

Aaron nodded and said, "Yeah, I guess she wouldn't do that."

Aaron thought for a minute, then asked, "How much did Stacy have to drink during your dinner?"

Richard thought for a minute, then stated, "We hadn't even finished dinner. We both had a glass of wine, but she still had half a glass left when she stormed out."

"Did you have any pre-dinner drinks?" Aaron asked.

Richard answered, "No. We had reservations, so we were seated shortly after arriving at the restaurant. I can say with certainty that she was not intoxicated during our argument nor when she left the restaurant."

Aaron then said, "Well, let's move on from there. Where were you early yesterday morning?"

Richard just stared.

Aaron explained, "You know the chief would not like it if I didn't ask that question. Sorry man, but I have to give him an answer. That thoroughness thing we talked about."

Richard cleared his throat, then answered, "The question itself borders on accusation. But I get it, I understand. You're right, it needs to be asked. But make no mistake about it, I may be guilty of lying to the chief about dinner with Stacy, but I am absolutely innocent about having anything to do with her death. If that is what you are insinuating."

"Early yesterday morning? I got a call at six o'clock from one of my clients, Frank Lewis. He had been in a bad accident just outside of town. Swerved to miss a deer and went off the road, down a short embankment, sideswiped a tree which knocked the vehicle onto its side. Scared him to death, as you might imagine. He was able to call 911 and get some help. Then he called me. So, I went to help him out."

Aaron listened intently, and then said, "I know about the accident, it happened right before my shift. The sheriff's department handled it. But I don't know any details. Been pretty busy since then with this case. Was he hurt? Was there anyone else in the car?"

Richard said, "No one else in the car. He had some bumps and bruises, but nothing serious. Chief Patrick and his fire crew checked him out at the scene, said he'd be very sore the next morning, but no need to go to the hospital. Tow truck was able to get the car out and taken to the shop. It was totaled."

Aaron said, "Just curious, do you usually go to the scene of every accident in which one of your clients is involved?" Aaron already knew the answer to this, but he wanted Richard to explain.

"No, not usually. Oftentimes I receive a call and talk them through the procedure of what to do, what information to get, how to contact the claims adjuster, that sort of thing. But Frank is not only an important customer, he's become a good friend. And this was not your typical fender-bender. He's sent me a lot of referrals over the few years I've been here, not to mention both of his children are also my customers. So, I went out, waited with him for the tow truck, chit-chatted with the fire crew, and then gave him a ride home." Richard explained.

"Good enough. Please understand, we have to cross all the t's and dot all the i's in every investigation. Of course, that means I will be calling Frank and Chief Patrick as part of my follow-up. But I just want to say, as far as we're concerned, you've got a good reputation in the community as well as at our department," Aaron concluded.

"Thanks Aaron. I appreciate that. I also appreciate you guys doing absolutely everything to catch whoever did this to Stacy," Richard said.

To change to a lighter subject, Aaron asked Richard if ol' lady Perkins was one of his customers. Richard explained that he had inherited her as a customer from his predecessor and then, as they finished their lunch, they talked about the Main Street Fountain she had created. When they finished eating, the waitress brought the tab and Richard quickly pulled out his credit card. Aaron said, "I appreciate the offer for you to pick up the tab, but the Chief has very strict policies concerning such things." He then dropped a twenty on top of the credit card and added, "This should be close enough. Thanks."

Richard nodded and said, "I understand." They shook hands and went to their respective offices.

Dani walked into the chief's office and said, "Hey Boss, yesterday I was surprised when you mentioned Dr. Clevenger as a possible suspect. But then today, during my interview with him, he said something that bothers me just a bit.

"What was that?" the chief asked.

Dani explained, "It's probably nothing, but, he made a comment about how rough Stacy's life had been lately and then added something about it might be a blessing that her life was over. That just seemed, I don't know, kind of a harsh statement. A blessing that her life was over? As if, her murder might be a blessing? It just seems to me to be a weird statement. I don't know, maybe like a Dr. Kovorkian attitude?"

The chief rolled the statement over in his mind and then said, "Yes, I see what you are saying. It might not have come out the way he intended it to come out. Nonetheless, it does seem a funny thing to say. And let's not forget, as a physician, he'd certainly know exactly where to stab someone if his intent was to kill."

"Exactly!" Dani replied.

The chief then asked, "How did the rest of his interview go?"

"No surprises. He explained why he was on Elm. He confirmed that he did talk to Mrs. Perkins. When prompted, he finally remembered the motorcycle, which he identified as a Harley. He checked out fine. It was that last statement of his that just doesn't sit well with me," Dani summarized.

"Well," the chief reasoned, "Usually, when your gut is trying to tell you something, it's worth considering. However, we can't build a case around that one statement. But let's not discard it. Let's not forget, he was on the street shortly before Josh found her body. For now, let's keep him as a suspect, not at the top of the list, but on the list nonetheless."

"Thanks Boss," Dani said as she walked out of the office.

At that moment, Aaron walked into the station. Like Dani, he too, was surprised to see Steve sitting in one of the cells. He looked at Steve for a moment and then nodded, Steve nodded back, then Aaron went straight into the chief's office.

"Got a minute?" he asked Chief Earl.

"Sure," the chief said.

Aaron began, "I'd like to debrief you on my interviews with Coach Stewart and with Richard White. Both were very interesting."

However, before they could continue, Michelle came to the chief's door and said, "Josh Allen is here, per your request."

The chief said to Aaron, "Let me deal with this, first. Then we'll talk."

He then turned to Michelle and said, "Have we heard from Michael at the coroner's office yet?"

"No. Not yet," Michelle replied.

"Check with Dani and see if we've had a response on IAFIS yet. But first, show Josh in, please."

Michelle said, "Sorry chief, Dani just left to go interview Dotty."

The chief replied, "Good. We can worry about the fingerprints later. Let me know when Dani gets back. Go ahead and send Josh in."

Chapter Eleven: Suspects

Josh walked hurriedly into the chief's office and said, "Okay Chief Earl, now can you please tell me why in the world Steve is in one of the cells?!"

"Sit down, Josh," the chief instructed. Josh sat and the chief continued, "You told me that Steve overslept yesterday morning and that's why he was late for work."

"Yes, that's correct. That's what he told me," Josh said.

"Well, he lied to you, and he lied to me about why he was late," the chief informed Josh.

"Okay. He shouldn't have lied. But if you put everyone who ever told a lie in jail, you'd have to build a lot more prisons," Josh said,

"Let me finish," the chief responded. "Steve didn't come clean about his lies on his own, there were witnesses who saw him early that morning, riding his motorcycle. Would you like to venture a guess as to where he was seen?"

"I have no idea," Josh answered.

The chief laid it all out, "He was seen on Elm Street, riding up the street from Stacy's house. That was just a short time before you found Stacy dead on her back porch. He was then two hours late for work. He lied to you as to why he was late. When I confronted him about it this morning, he lied a second time about why he was late. Are you starting to get the picture here, Josh? Now do you understand why Steve is sitting in my cell?"

Josh looked stunned, and then muttered, "Wow. This looks really bad."

To which the chief replied, "Well, bad just went to worse. After being confronted about his lies, Steve now admits that he was on Elm Street early yesterday morning, but he refuses to tell me why he was there. He says he can't because it's a private matter. A private matter! That boy better get a lot smarter real fast or he's heading for a world of trouble."

Josh stared at the chief for a moment or two, trying to process everything he had just heard. He then responded,

"Chief, can I talk to him in private please? Maybe I can find out what the heck he is talking about."

The chief ran his fingers through his hair and replied, "Well Josh, that's what I had in mind when I asked you to come down here. He's been sitting there for a couple of hours now. Maybe that has given him time to think a little more clearly. I'll have Eric show you both to the conference room and you can talk in private with him in there."

When they were situated in the conference room, Josh said to Steve, "Wow, man. You look absolutely terrible."

"Yeah, thanks for the word of encouragement," Steve responded.

"I'm sorry. But what the heck is going on? The chief said all you have to do is explain why you were on your bike on Elm yesterday morning and you can go home. What's the deal? AND, why did you lie to me about oversleeping? What's that all about?"

Steve explained, "It's all about the same thing. Like I told the chief, it's a private thing and I can't talk about it to anyone. I lied to you because I had to. I didn't want to. I had to. I'm sorry, but I had no choice."

"You always have a choice. You have a choice right now! Let's forget about you lying to me. That's not the most important thing here. Why can't you just tell the chief why you were on Elm yesterday? Let's get the heck out of here and get back to work," Josh pleaded.

"I wish it were that easy, Josh, I really do. But I can't tell anybody why I was riding my bike home so early in the morning," Steve said.

Josh quickly replied, "Anybody? I'm not just anybody. You're my best friend. I thought I was your best friend. At least tell me what you've gotten yourself into. Maybe I can help!"

Steve stared at his friend, then at the ground, then tried to explain, "I got myself into this mess. I just have to ride it out. As soon as the chief catches Stacy's killer, this will all go away. But I absolutely cannot say why I was on Elm yesterday. Not a chance."

Out of frustration, Josh slammed his hand on the table and stood. He leaned toward Steve and responded intensely, "Look you idiot, as far as I know, they have no leads in this case. You are the closest thing they have to a suspect! They think they have motive because of your past history with Stacy. They think they have opportunity because of you being right there at the right time. This isn't just going to go away. If they are convinced you are the murderer, they may not even pursue any other options."

Steve took a heavy breath and with a tormented look, said, "Buddy, I do not know what to do! This is the worst mess I've ever gotten into in my life. The only thing I know right now is that I absolutely cannot explain why I was there. There are consequences for saying anything more."

Josh expounded, "There are worse consequences for not saying anything at all."

"Still, for right now, I have nothing more I can say," Steve replied.

"Fine! Have it your way! They're going to put you back in the cell. I think the chief may have to charge you pretty soon. I'll ask if I can stop by first thing in the morning. If you want to talk, if you need anything, ask them to call me," Josh said.

"Thanks a bunch for stopping by. Don't give up on me, okay?" Steve said tentatively.

"Never," Josh replied. He stared at his friend for a moment and then let out a long sigh. "Never," he repeated.

Josh opened the door and signaled to Eric that they had finished. Then Steve whispered to Josh, "Hey, you never even asked me if I killed her."

Josh smiled, for the first time, and said, "I know you'd never do that. I don't need to ask."

Steve simply said, "Thanks, pal." They gave each other a big hug, and then Steve was taken back to the cell.

Josh went into the chief's office, shook his head and said, "Sorry Chief Earl. I tried, but he won't open up to me either. I know in my heart that he'd never hurt Stacy, I just can't figure out why he won't tell us why he was on Elm yesterday."

"I'm sorry to hear that, Josh. We'll let him sleep on it and see if we can persuade him in the morning. I can't detain him indefinitely without charging him. It's just a matter of time before I've got to take action," the chief said.

"I understand. I sure wouldn't want to be in your shoes. Would it be okay if I came by in the morning and talked to him again?" Josh asked.

"That's a good idea," the chief said, "See you at eight o'clock tomorrow morning.

"Thanks Chief, see you in the morning," Josh said. He then shook the chief's hand and walked out of the office.

After Josh left his office, the chief asked Aaron to come in and debrief him on his visits with Coach Stewart and with Richard White.

He began with his visit with the coach, "I know it's not very professional, but I've got to say it right up front, that coach has become a bona fide idiot. I used to look up to him. Now, I can hardly stand the sight of him. Has he changed that much, or have I?"

The chief chuckled and then said, "Well, we all change. That includes both of you. But I must say, the coach has indeed changed a lot these last few years, and not for the better. He's gotten far worse than just being a little rough around the edges. It's a shame, because he did a lot of good for a lot of kids over the years. I hate to see that legacy ruined during the few years he has left as a coach."

"Well put, Chief. If only someone could sit down and have a heart to heart talk with him. I'm just not sure if there is anyone he'd even listen to anymore," Aaron wondered.

"Sadly, probably not. But we need to get back to the case. How did the interview go?" the chief asked.

"First of all, the coach has a spear standing in the corner of his office!" Aaron proclaimed.

"A spear! You've got to be kidding me. Did you ask him about it?" the chief questioned.

"I didn't have to ask. I've actually held that spear. I know all about it," Aaron responded.

"Continue," the chief demanded.

"It's called the Spirit Spear. During the football season, after each game the coaches select the defensive player of the game. That player has proven to be the point of the spear of the defense, so to speak. He then gets the honor of leading the team onto the field at the next game. He carries the spear with him, held high in the air. Eventually he thrusts it into the ground on the football field and the players jump, yell and scream as they get fired up for the game. It's a tradition that goes back many years. In fact, in my playing days here, I actually was lucky enough to carry the spear before one of our games," Aaron explained.

"I bet luck had nothing to do with it, just good solid football skills," the chief praised.

"Well, I don't know about that, but I remember it to this day. It sure fires up the defense, as well as the rest of the team and even the fans," Aaron said.

"So, Coach Stewart has a spear in his office. The very type of weapon we are looking for. He didn't happen to mention the last time the spear was out of his office did he? You didn't notice any blood on it, did you?" the chief inquired.

"I looked it over and didn't see any blood. But, of course, he would have cleaned it off. But more importantly, he said he was in his office from six-thirty all yesterday morning," Aaron answered.

"She could have been murdered before six-thirty. Until we establish the time of death, we still need to confirm his alibi from six-thirty on. Any witnesses see him there?" the chief asked.

"I was about to ask that exact question when the bell rang and he had to get to his next class. It wasn't exactly a friendly discussion at that point, so he refused to stick around for just a question or two more. I plan on going back tomorrow to follow up," Aaron explained.

"If that spear isn't in his office when you go in tomorrow, you slap the cuffs on him and immediately bring him in. If the spear is still there, ask your question about witnesses. If he changes his story and he has no witnesses, bring him in for further questioning. And bring that spear in, too! It obviously could be a key piece of evidence in the case. On the other hand, if he has any witnesses, follow-up immediately with them and see if they confirm his alibi," the chief instructed.

"Will do, Chief," Aaron said.

"Even if he was there at six-thirty, that doesn't get him off the suspect list. We need to get a timeline established as soon as possible," the chief reasoned. "Meanwhile, how did it go with Richard?"

"Richard and I actually had lunch together," Aaron began, "and we had a very good discussion. He's a good man, trying to do the right thing, loves his community, striving to be a good agent for his clients. But he's hurting, big time. He was quick to confess that he lied to you about the last time he had seen Stacy, and he regrets telling that lie. In fact, he offered to apologize to you in person."

"Then why tell the lie in the first place?" the chief interrupted.

"Embarrassment, essentially. Totally embarrassed about a public argument in the restaurant. That and the fact that he was emotionally devastated after hearing of Stacy's death. Didn't have a clear head when he responded. A stupid mistake. But here's the important part. He was at an accident scene early yesterday morning. One of his clients totaled his car and called Richard for help. He left his home around six and didn't get back until later."

"Other than his client, any credible witnesses to confirm his presence at the accident?" the chief asked.

"How's this for credible? Chief Patrick was at the scene," Aaron said.

"Have you confirmed this with Gary?" The chief asked.

"Not yet, but I'll call him as soon as we're done," Aaron said.

"That's okay. I'll give him a call. Bottom line then is that both Coach Stewart and Richard White have early morning alibis. Coach Stewart could only have committed the murder if it occurred before six-thirty, and Richard only if it occurred before six o'clock. Therefore, if we determine the time of death to be before six o'clock, both are still high on the list. If it occurred after six-thirty, both are off the list.

Unfortunately, we don't yet know how early the murder occurred," The chief summarized.

"Yes, sir. Pending Chief Patrick's confirmation of Richard's story," Aaron agreed.

"Good work Aaron. So, we have those two as plausible suspects, but for my money, Steve stays at the top of our list," the chief stated.

"Yeah, what's that all about?" Aaron asked.

The chief answered, "Simple. First, he lied about sleeping in that morning, but he now admits to being on Elm. He was seen riding his motorcycle up the street from her house, but he refuses to tell us why he was on Elm in the first place. He was two hours late to work, work which was, in fact, at her very house. As a former boyfriend, he has a past history with her. Individually, all weak points at this time. But, when taken together, it begins to look like the start for building a case. It's all we have to go on for now. Lots more work to be done."

Aaron shrugged his shoulders and said, "Yep, lots more to do." He then stood and left the chief's office.

The chief picked up his phone and asked Michelle to get Chief Patrick on the line for him. Fire Chief Gary Patrick had lived in Springerville just a year and a half longer than Chief Earl. He was an Irish African American who stood five foot nine inches tall. His short-cropped, salt and pepper hair only covered the sides and back of his head, leaving the top of his head shiny and bald. He had worked for the Atlanta, Georgia fire department before moving to Springerville. He and his wife, Cathy, whom he married a week after graduating from high school, had discussed on several occasions the hope of moving to a smaller town in which to raise their three children, Barbara, Chad and Jessi. Through a friend, he had heard about a position out of state, in a little town called Springerville. The fire department was looking for an engineer at the time. He and Cathy did some research on the town and then he applied for the job. Upon being hired, he began working there as an engineer on the firetruck. In addition to driving the truck and making sure it was properly supplied and ready to go at all times, on the scene of a fire he was also in charge of making sure the water was pumped properly from the truck through the hoses or from the hydrant to the truck. This was in addition to performing all the duties of the rest of the firefighters. He was also second in command to the fire chief.

He had been there eight years when the position of Chief opened up. He was the only one from the Springerville Department to apply, while two other candidates from out of state also applied. After a series of tests and interviews, Chief Patrick was hired.

Over the years Chief Patrick and Chief Earl had worked together on many occasions. The fact that both of them had come from larger cities to a smaller town was only one of the things they had in common. Chief Earl had served in the army, Chief Patrick served in the air force as a fighter jet mechanic. They both had an outstanding reputation, not only from those in their departments, but also from the townsfolk in general. They both attended the same non-denominational Christian Church and had served on the church's building committee when they built their new sanctuary. They had both also participated in a short-term mission trip to the Dominican Republic, working with the less fortunate in that country. Their wives had struck up a friendship as they got to know each other while singing in the church choir.

Of no little significance, both Fred and Gary loved fishing. Specifically, trout fishing. The two of them had spent many a day chasing trout around the lake. Sometimes just the two of them, oftentimes with their wives. Occasionally, another individual or couple would join them. But, more often than not, it was the two of them, enjoying their fishing, loving the outdoors, telling jokes, sitting around a campfire teasing each other, but most of all, relaxing, away from the stress of their jobs. Simply stated, they had become best friends, and they both cherished that friendship.

Chief Earl sat in his office just a minute or two when Michelle buzzed him and said, "Chief Patrick on one, sir."

The chief said, "Thanks Michelle."

He then pushed the button for line one and said, "Hey Gary, why aren't you out putting out fires? What are we paying you for anyway!?"

The fire chief laughed and replied, "Did they have to wake you from your nap so you could call me?"

Chief Earl said, "If I could sneak in a nap once in a while, I wouldn't be so grumpy!"

"Nah," Chief Patrick countered, "You were born grumpy and have spent the better part of your life perfecting it."

After their good-natured teasing, Chief Earl said, "Hey, quick question for you. Did you happen to see Richard White at an accident scene early yesterday morning?"

"Yep, sure did," the chief replied. "Around five forty-five one of his customers decided to play chicken with a deer and lost. Went down a slope, then lost an encounter with a tree and ended up with his car on its side. Fortunately, the guy wasn't hurt. But yes, Richard was there. We talked for a while and when we left Richard was still there, the two of them waiting for a tow truck. Why do you ask?"

"Just confirming his story. I figured the guy had to be desperate if he was using you for his alibi!" the chief again teased.

"No doubt!" Chief Patrick shot back. "But I'm sure glad I was able to help you do your job, once again!"

"Oh, you're quick. Hey seriously, thanks for the info. Stay safe out there," Chief Earl replied.

Chief Patrick said, "You too, buddy. Hey Fred, while I've got you on the phone, Cathy asked me to see if you and Diane could come over for dinner Saturday night. I'll throw a few steaks on the grill, pull the cork on a bottle of Merlot, and we can tell each other some lies about our last fishing trip. Say, six o'clock?"

Chief Earl quickly went back to his teasing mode, "Some more of your burned steaks and cheap wine?"

Chief Patrick laughed and replied, "Hey, cheapskate, you are more than welcome to bring the wine."

Chief Earl smiled as he said, "Well, that's what I get for opening my big mouth. We will be happy to bring a bottle of the fruit of the vine. And we look forward to your delicious steaks, or do you want me to bring those as well? Seriously, it sounds good. I'll confirm with Diane and we'll plan on it. Thanks a bunch Gary. See you Saturday."

The chief smiled as he hung up. He then turned and looked at a picture of himself and his good friend, Gary Patrick, a picture of them holding up a nice stringer of fish which they had caught the previous summer. "We're way overdue for another long trip," he thought to himself. He decided the planning for the next trip would begin Saturday evening in Gary's back yard.

The chief then called Aaron back into his office. He said, "Chief Patrick just confirmed Richard's alibi."

"No surprise there," Aaron observed.

"Aaron," the chief continued, "Let me run something by you."

"Sure thing," Aaron quickly replied.

The chief explained, "Do you remember seeing Mike Lambeau on Main Street when Mrs. Perkins backed into the fire hydrant?"

Aaron thought for a minute and then said, "No, I can't say that I do."

"I didn't see him either," the chief continued, "It seems to me that, although it wasn't earth shattering news, that's a story he would cover. Great photo opportunity for the paper. It isn't every day you see a fountain like that on Main Street."

"Good point," Aaron said.

"Furthermore," the chief observed, "He got to Stacy's almost immediately after we got there."

"Yes, that's true," Aaron said, "He said that he heard it on his scanner, and came over."

The chief responded, "Okay, but he got there before Dani and at about the same time that Eric got there. That is very quick! Makes me wonder if he was already in the area? And he was relentless with his questions; borderline rude, almost obsessive."

"Hmmm," Aaron pondered, "I hadn't thought of that. Good observations, Boss. It sure makes one start to wonder. In fact, now that I think about it, he was hammering me with questions at the scene. He's also called me twice trying to get more information. He's either relentless as a reporter or he has an unhealthy interest in this case."

"Indeed," said the chief, "Perhaps a personal interest. Furthermore, Dani saw him in the neighborhood after she finished up her interview with Mrs. Perkins. Of course, there could be many reasons for him to be there, but it sure seems coincidental."

Aaron asked, "Do you think we need to rattle his cage a bit?"

"Leave no stone unturned. I'm going to send Eric over to have a conversation with Mike and see what he can discover," the chief stated.

"You know, ever since Eric wrote Mike a ticket for speeding out on the highway, they just don't get along too well," Aaron reminded the chief.

"Exactly," the chief replied, "Perhaps that antagonism can serve as a slight distraction and work to our favor."

Aaron smiled as he replied, "Sounds good."

He then paused for a moment, but then said, "Chief, I hesitate to say this, but I believe it needs to be said. Since we're talking about an additional suspect, I believe there should be one more name on our list. I think we've ignored the obvious."

"I'm thinking the same thing," the chief agreed, "Although, his is the last name I'd ever expect to be on a suspect list."

Aaron quickly opined, "I agree. For the life of me though, I can't think of any motive."

"Things aren't always what they seem to be," the chief stated. He then added, "It might also explain Steve's refusal to talk about his presence on Elm yesterday morning. Perhaps he stumbled onto something. Something that would put him in a horrible predicament. Something that might cause him to keep saying 'it's a private matter.'"

"Do you want me to bring him in for questioning?" Aaron asked.

The chief thought for a moment, then he nodded and directed, "Yes, it's time we address the issue. Go pick up Josh Allen."

Chapter Twelve: Best Friends

Dani had set an appointment with Dotty for mid-afternoon. Dotty didn't seem too interested in meeting with the detective, but as the chief had instructed, Dani was persistent.

Dani agreed to meet Dotty at her hair salon, "Elite Short Cuts." Located just a block off of Main Street, the salon derived its name from Dotty's stature, or lack thereof. She was a petite lady with a big, bubbly personality. She was quick to laugh, quick to tease, quick to be teased, but also very quick to have empathy for another. Her spunky attitude and petite stature earned her the honor of being at the top of the high school cheerleader pyramids. She loved the attention it brought her and cherished being on the cheerleading squad, not only because of the friends who were on the squad, but also because of the social status it brought her in high school.

Upon graduation from high school, she enrolled in Cosmetology School which was located not far from the same small college Stacy attended. They had shared an apartment there, that is, until Stacy moved in with Shane. Dotty eventually found another roommate, but it just wasn't the same as rooming with Stacy.

Upon completion of her program, she returned to Springerville and began working in one of the local beauty salons. After a few years, the owner of the salon decided to retire. Although there were a few older ladies who had worked as hair stylists much longer than Dotty, none of them were interested in owning the salon. Thus, when the owner approached Dotty with an offer to sell her the salon, Dotty jumped at the chance.

She paid half of the agreed upon purchase price up front with a loan secured from her parents. The balance would be paid in monthly installments over a six year period. And just like that, Dotty became the very proud owner of the Springerville tHAIRapy Salon. Having never liked the name to begin with, Dotty quickly changed it to

Elite Short Cuts. After a fresh coat of paint and some minor remodeling of the salon, she had her Grand Opening. Her ever optimistic and often animated attitude was infectious and the ladies, and one gentleman, who worked in the salon enjoyed the lively attitude of the salon, as well as a new generation of customers.

When Dani arrived at the salon, Dotty was at the front desk, on the phone finalizing an appointment for one of the salon's many clients. Her usual effervescent expression seemed to fade just a bit when she saw Dani walk in. She finished her conversation and then said to Dani, with what Dani thought to be a somewhat forced smile, "Good afternoon Dani, I hope you are having a wonderful day. Why don't we step into my office? We'll be more comfortable there."

She led the way to her office and closed the door behind them. She offered Dani a glass of water, Perrier, which Dani politely declined.

Dotty then commented, "So, you wanted to ask me about my best friend, Stacy."

"Yes," Dani replied. "Thank you for taking time to talk with me."

Dotty quickly said, "But of course! No one knew Stacy better than I, and if there is anything at all that I can do to help you investigate this horrible, horrible crime, I will help in any way I can."

She then reached for a tissue and dabbed her eyes. Before Dani could ask her first question, Dotty continued, "Stacy and I have been best friends since high school. We were inseparable. I was maid of honor in her wedding. We roomed together in college. We were like sisters. I was at the hospital when both of her children were born. In fact, we have been neighbors now for a few years. I can't imagine not having her in my life."

She paused to dab her eyes again and Dani quickly said, "Neighbors? I didn't know you live on Elm Street."

Dotty furrowed her brow, and then explained, "No, no. I don't live next to her. I live BEHIND her. On Maple street.

We even put in a little gate in our back yard fence so that we could visit each other easier."

Dani said, "Wow. That is close. So, you really were like sisters. You might say, she was like your older sister?"

Dotty stared at Dani for a moment and then slowly explained, "No. We're the same age. We graduated from high school the same year."

Dani interjected, "Yeah, of course, I get that. I just meant because of her popularity and her being the captain of the cheerleading squad and all of that. Maybe it was like an older sister - younger sister relationship. But maybe that's a bad description. We'll just leave it as sisters."

Dotty, frustrated, tried to explain, "Look, everybody loved Stacy. We all know that! The girls all wanted to be her friend, as if some of her popularity would rub off on them. The teachers all treated her like a princess. The boys all fawned all over her, as if any of them stood a chance. Except, of course, Shane."

Dani again interrupted Dotty, "Tell me. How did you and Shane get along?"

Dani wasn't sure, but it seemed to her that Dotty's countenance changed just a bit with that question.

Dotty calmly said, "Perhaps you didn't know that Shane and I dated before he dated Stacy?"

Dani replied, "No, I didn't know that. I had no idea. That had to hurt a bit."

"What do you mean?" demanded Dotty.

"I'm sorry. I'm not trying to open up old hurt feelings. Perhaps, I should ask about something else?" Dani replied.

"No, go ahead. You have a question about hurt feelings? What hurt feelings are you talking about?" Dotty demanded.

"Maybe I misunderstood the timing of the whole thing. When you said you and Shane were dating before he started dating Stacy, I assumed that he had left you to start dating her. If so, I would think that had to hurt, especially if she was your best friend. But, maybe there was some time between you dating him and Stacy dating him?"

"No," Dotty coldly responded. "Shane actually broke up with me to start dating her. There, is that what you wanted to know? This seems like an interview for a gossip magazine instead of question about a person who was just murdered. That was a long, long time ago. I don't see how we got on this topic at all."

Not wanting to let his issue go just yet, Dani quickly continued, "Again, I don't mean to open up any old wounds. If I have, I am deeply sorry, Dotty. I was only responding to your statement that you and Stacy were best friends. I believe you said that you were inseparable, like sisters. I guess it was more of an observation than a question; you must have had a very unique relationship to stay best friends even after Shane dumped you to date Stacy."

Dani knew that the term "dumped" was a bit harsh, but her gut was telling her that deep down, Dotty really wanted to address this issue. Perhaps it was an issue that never had truly been resolved. So, she pushed just a little.

Dotty then very slowed explained, "Shane and I dated before Stacy came along and turned on her charm. She knew that we were together, but she didn't care. What could I do? She was Stacy! I didn't have a chance. Plus, she was my friend. That was a friendship everyone wanted and I had it. So, I just kept my mouth shut and acted like losing Shane to her was no big deal. All along I knew she wasn't right for him. She never appreciated him. She loved the idea of being married to him, his image, his reputation; but she never completely loved him! Not like I love him. I mean, "loved," while we were dating."

Dotty stopped herself and grabbed another tissue. Dani, realizing that this interview had just entered a whole new level, was being very careful how she would phrase her next question.

"Dotty," Dani slowly asked, "Are you and Shane still friends? With all that has happened between him and Stacy, did your friendship with Shane end, or do you still consider him to be a friend?"

Dotty looked surprised at the question as she answered, "Of course we're friends. We've all been friends since high school. Oftentimes I help transfer the kids back and forth between Shane and Stacy. Through all of their ups and downs, I've been a faithful friend to both of them."

Dani asked, "And Stacy never minded that you were friends with Shane, even during the divorce?"

"No," Dotty explained, "but I didn't rub her face in it."

"I'm not sure what you mean," Dani pushed.

"Look, this isn't public information, but Shane and I started seeing each other a few months ago. In fact, we are still seeing each other. But I didn't want that to be an awkward situation with Stacy, so we've kept it quiet," Dotty explained.

"If I may ask, what is the status of that relationship now?" Dani questioned. Again, she thought she noticed a change in Dotty's continence as she paused and pondered her question before speaking.

"That's a great question!" Dotty said indignantly, "Things were going just fine until, for some strange reason, Stacy decided that she might want to see if she and Shane had a chance of getting back together. Can you believe it!?

They're divorced. Why can't she just get over it and let it go?!"

Dani was stunned. She quickly blurted out, "But what about Richard. I thought that Richard and Stacy were an item."

"So did I. So did everyone else. But that's how Stacy has always worked. If she sees something she wants, nothing and no one stands in her way," Dotty fumed, "Besides, she and Richard never really got along. They argued all the time, but stayed together. I think she was just staying in a relationship with Richard until something better came along."

She then quickly realized that she had said much, much more than she had planned on saying. She was mad at Dani for asking so many questions, but ever madder at herself for saying so much, perhaps, too much.

Dani was anxious to ask a few more pertinent questions, but then, the door suddenly opened and Brittany, one of Dotty's stylists, poked her head into the office and said, "Hey Dotty, your next appointment is here.

She's been waiting ten minutes. Should I try to reschedule?"

Dotty said, "No, I'll be right there. We're done here." She then took yet another tissue to blow her nose. She stood and looked in the mirror on the wall and dabbed at her mascara.

Desperately, Dani said, "Dotty, I have a few more questions. Please, just a couple of minutes."

Dotty glared at her and said, "I have clients waiting. I have a business to run. You'll have to come back." With that, she walked out of the room. As she approached her client, she put on a big smile and enthusiastically said, "Betty, how good to see you. I'm so sorry to keep you waiting. Wow, that's a beautiful sweater you're wearing today. Is that new?"

Dani closed her notebook, walked out the door, and drove immediately back to the police station.

Andrea answered the phone when Aaron called Josh's home. When Andrea informed him that Josh was not home yet, Aaron asked if Andrea knew where he was. She informed him that yes, she did know, and then proceeded to give him the address. Aaron thanked her, hung up the phone, and went to his squad car. He then drove over to the work sight. When he arrived, he saw Josh loading a circular saw into the back storage box of his pickup truck.

As Aaron got out of his car, Josh looked up and said, "Hi Aaron. How's Steve doing? You guys still got him locked up?"

"That's why I'm here, Josh," Aaron explained, "The chief has another question or two he'd like to ask you if you wouldn't mind coming down to the station."

"I already told him I'd stop by in the morning. Is this something that can wait until then?" Josh asked.

Aaron explained, "This is a huge case, Josh. There's a ton of information we're having to sift through. We want to catch this person as soon as possible. We sure don't want a murderer roaming the streets of Springerville. The chief just has a couple of quick questions, if you could swing by when you're done here."

"Sure thing," Josh replied, "In fact, I'm done here for today. Let me finish packing up and I'll be there in about fifteen minutes."

Aaron said, "Sounds good. Thanks." He then got back in his car and drove away.

Chapter Thirteen: Innocent, But Guilty?

Michelle knocked on the chief's door and he motioned her in. He was just finishing up a call from another reporter. He had learned a long time ago how to say a lot without really saying very much at all.

Michelle said, "Dr. Terrace just called and said he has just finished his preliminary examination of Stacy. He said to tell you that she died from a single stab wound in her chest. The instrument sliced the aorta artery which caused her to bleed to death. He said the wound looked more like it had been caused by a spear than a knife. He said that he was not saying it was a spear, but that the wound was similar in appearance to what a spear wound would look like. He said there were no other marks, bruises or cuts on her body. He also said if you had any other questions, he would be happy to take your call."

The chief pondered her statement, then said, "Something like a spear. Wow! Thanks Michelle. Please call Michael back and ask if he would send a blood sample up to the County Medical Examiner's Office right away so that they can establish a DNA record for future reference. Also, please ask if he was able to establish a time of death."

"I'll do so immediately," she replied.

The chief called Eric into his office and asked, "How is that time line coming along? That is critical to narrowing the window in regards to time of death."

Eric replied, "Just about done. Unfortunately, we know she was at the restaurant the night before, but we have no one who saw her before Josh found her on the patio. Theoretically, she could have died any time between ten the previous evening and eight that morning. It's a very large window. But there is something else I want to check out. When Dani and I canvassed the neighborhood, there were a few homes where no one answered the door. I thought it might be beneficial to go back and see if we can pick up any additional information."

"Absolutely! Get right on it," the chief directed.

Michelle again walked into the chief's office. She said, "The FBI called while you were talking to Eric. No hits on the finger print search."

"I expected that would be what we got. But we have to cover all the bases. Thanks," the chief replied.

Aaron entered as Michelle exited the office. He said, "Boss, Josh will be here in about 15 minutes."

The chief nodded, then explained, "When he gets here I want to talk to him twice. First, about Steve. Then I'll have him talk to Steve. When's he's done, bring him back in. I'll see if he's had any luck getting Steve to open up. Then I'll ask about his whereabouts yesterday morning before he called us."

"Will do," Aaron said.

The chief then went to the cell to talk to Steve. He opened the door, went in, and sat next to Steve on the bed.

He said, "Steve, it is critical that you tell me why you were on Elm street yesterday morning. When I say critical, I mean that in the most severe sense of the word and I mean it in regards to you. It is extremely critical for you to tell me why you were there."

Steve did not hesitate to respond, "Chief Earl, I'm sorry but I absolutely cannot tell you why I was there."

The chief stared at him and Steve looked away. The chief then said, "Suit yourself Steve. I sincerely hope you don't later regret taking this stance."

He then walked out, locked the door to the cell, and went back to his office.

Ten minutes later, Josh was shown into the chief's office. The chief looked up and said, "Hello Josh, please take a seat."

As he sat down, Josh said, "I see you are still holding Steve. How long do you plan on doing that?"

The chief replied, "Until he can explain why he was seen on Stacy's street at or near the time of her murder. When people feel the need to lie to the law, there's a reason for that lie, and the reason is never a good one."

"Well," Josh rationalized, "I'm sure he has a good reason."

"Tell you what," the chief offered, "why don't you go in again and try to convince Steve to tell you why? One justifiable reason, and he walks out of here. Why not see if you can talk some sense into him?"

Josh puffed out his cheeks, then said, "Sure. Let me try again." He was then shown to the cell where Steve was sitting on a cot.

"Hey buddy, how's the outside world today?" Steve quipped.

"It's still there, waiting for you to join it," Josh replied, "And I must say, you seem rather chipper for a guy who just spent the better part of the day in a cell."

Steve smiled and said, "What do you want me to do? Start banging a tin cup on the bars of the cell or break out a rendition of 'Old Man River?' It's not like I have a choice here."

"That's exactly the point," Josh growled as he held his arms out to his sides, palms up, "You DO have a choice! Just tell the chief why you were on Elm when you said you were home in bed!"

Steve leaned forward and said, "I told you. I CAN'T give the reason as to why I was there. Someone else will be hurt if I do. I will not ruin someone else's life because of my problem. Whatever happens, happens, and I'll just have to deal with it."

Josh pointed at Steve and responded, "You are making absolutely no sense at all. You're willing to be a suspect in a murder because you want to keep a secret? Whoever that somebody else is and whatever that somebody else did, nothing is as bad as being charged with a murder."

"It's not that simple," Steve replied.

"Wait a minute, are you trying to tell me that you know who killed Stacy and now you've got to protect them? Please tell me you realize that can make you an accomplice to murder or maybe obstruction of justice or who knows what else?" Josh challenged.

Steve explained, "No. I have no idea who killed Stacy. My riding my bike on Elm had absolutely nothing to do with her murder. The reason for riding my bike on Elm involves another person and their right to privacy. Their right to not have their life destroyed, potentially. I just can't drag someone else down with me."

"Again," Josh pleaded as he stood and looked down at Steve, "You are making no sense whatsoever. Look, if you can't tell the chief, at least tell me. I give you my word, I won't tell him or anyone else. After all we've been through, you can't even confide in me what's going on so that I can at least try to help figure something out? Best friends help each other out, but they can't do that unless they trust each other."

Steve thought for a moment about what Josh had said. He did feel the need to tell someone what had happened. He felt terrible about the whole thing. He also reasoned that maybe Josh could come up with a way out of this mess.

Josh sat down as Steve began, "First, If, and I do mean IF, I tell you, do you swear not to tell a living soul, not even the chief? I need your word on that. You take it to your grave."

"Yes. I give you my word," Josh said hopefully.

Steve continued, "Okay. With your promise to keep this between you and me, I'll tell you the critical part, but I will not name names."

"Fair enough," Josh nodded."

"I was at Ron's Bar and Grille the night before. Shooting pool, knocking back a few drinks, just having fun. Couple of guys there, couple of gals there. Good times. Comes closing time and I'm invited over to a certain female's home, just for another drink or two. I followed her home on my bike, didn't leave until early the next morning. I did not spend the night on Elm Street, but my route home from her place took me up Elm Street. That's why I can't tell the chief my reason for being on Elm Street."

Josh thought for a moment and then said, "Look, knucklehead. Your sad social life notwithstanding, you are a single guy and I doubt that the chief is going to be shocked at your questionable moral standards."

Steve glared at Josh and said, "I'm single, but SHE isn't. Her husband was out of town on a business trip. He gets back into town this evening. I tell the chief what went on and he's going to want to confirm my alibi. He will probably have to put it in his police report. He may have one of his detectives talk to her husband to confirm that he was indeed out of town and oh, by the way did you know your wife was 'entertaining' in your absence. I did something incredibly stupid. I admit that. Blame it on the booze or stupidity or loneliness or whatever. I'm the idiot. I deserve whatever I get. But I will not drag her down with me. I will not ruin her marriage. I may be void of morals, but at least I have that. I'm not willing to destroy her life, no matter what it costs me. The bottom line is, I'm innocent in regards to Stacy, but I'm guilty as hell as to where I was that night. So, I've got to live with that guilt and its consequences."

Josh was stunned. He looked at Steve and was silent. After a moment he slowly said, "Wow."

Steve replied, "Yeah. Wow."

Josh asked, "How long have you been seeing her?"

Steve shook his head and replied, "It was only that one time. We've been friends for a while, but just friends. Until this happened. One night stand with a married woman. Stupid, stupid mistake. But I'm going to own the mistake. She made one little mistake, with my help, and I'm not going to be the reason her marriage blows up."

Josh leaned in toward Steve and said, "Look at me. Any woman who is hanging out at a bar at closing time and invites another man over to her house while her husband is out of town was on the prowl, just looking for trouble. Her marriage is already destined for failure, it's just a matter of time. I seriously doubt that you were her first fling and you won't be her last fling. For that kind of a woman, it's never a onetime deal."

"That kind of a woman!" Steve shot back, "You don't even know who she is."

"I know all I need to know," Josh replied.

In a mixture of anger and frustration, Steve expounded, "What you don't know is that she is a well-respected person in this community. They have four children. I absolutely, positively will NOT drag her marriage and her family into this mess!"

The two of them sat silently for a few minutes, not looking at each other.

Josh then said, "Hey look. Tell the chief that you can only answer if it is in strict confidence. That you will only answer if he doesn't tell anyone, ever, as to the reason. He's a standup kind of guy. He may not like what you did, but he'll then know why you were on Elm."

"Do you really think that a police chief investigating a murder is going to make a promise to a suspect to keep a secret in regards to his alibi?! Because I don't. I don't think he can. I simply can't take that risk," Steve argued. Then he continued, "It took all I have to trust you with this. And you are the only person on the planet I would trust. I'm glad I told you, because I want you to understand why I can't say anything. I want you to understand. That's important to me. But I'm not about to destroy her life because of what the rest of the world thinks of me. Telling the chief or anyone else cannot end well for her."

Josh couldn't think of anything else to say, so he simply said, "Okay."

Steve then smiled and said, "Cheer up, bud! I have a great plan."

Josh quipped, "Seriously?"

"Yep," Steve said, "My plan is that our great chief of police is going to quickly solve this crime and then he will have to let me out of here. Meanwhile, I've got free room and board and a very uncomfortable cot!"

Josh couldn't help but laugh, and then said, "You're still a knucklehead."

To which Steve replied, "That's Mr. Knucklehead to you!"

Josh was let out of the cell and returned to the chief's office. As he walked into the office, Chief Earl said to Josh, "Well?"

Josh shrugged his shoulders and said, "He's not going to budge. Insists that it's a private matter."

"Then, for now, he stays in the cell," the chief replied.

He then changed the subject, "Josh, do you mind if I ask you a question or two real quick?"

"Not at all," Josh replied. The chief motioned to a chair, and Josh took a seat.

But, before the chief could ask his question, Dani walked into his office and said, "Chief, I need to tell you something."

The chief said, "I'm in the middle of something. You'll have to wait until I'm done here."

Dani replied with urgency, "But this is very important information about an earlier interview."

The chief sternly replied, "This is also a very important interview. So, unless someone out there has a gun to someone's head, I'll talk to you when I'm finished here."

"Yes sir," Dani said dejectedly, and closed the door.

Josh said, "Chief, we can talk later if you'd like."

"Not a problem," the chief said, "This will only take a minute or two. What time did you arrive at Stacy's house?"

"Eight o'clock," Josh answered quickly.

"And where were you before you got to her house?" The chief asked.

"What do you mean?" Josh asked, somewhat confused.

"Well, did you go from your house straight to her house? If so, how long did that take?" the chief asked.

Josh stared at the chief for a moment, then, in disbelief he asked, "Are you questioning me as a source of information or as a suspect?"

"Please Josh, just answer the question," the chief said.

"Chief Earl, you've got my best friend locked up in a jail cell, even though I am one hundred percent certain that he has done nothing to deserve it, and now you are considering me a suspect in a murder case. This is insane! This is like a nightmare. Why in the world are you wasting your time harassing us when there's a murderer out there roaming the streets of our town?!"

The chief held up his hand and said, "Josh, please calm down and let me explain. It is no easy thing to ask you, of all people, these kinds of questions. I'm sorry to have to put you through this, but the fact is YOU are the one who found her body, you were all by yourself when you found her body. Additionally, your best friend was supposed to meet you at her house that morning. He was seen riding his motorcycle away from her house, but lied about even being on her street. When questioned, he states that he lied because it's a 'private matter." If his silence is not to protect himself, I have to wonder who he is protecting? Who would he care about so much that to protect that person, he'd risk being charged with murder? Is his silence an act of loyalty to his best friend?

So you see, there are questions that have to be asked of you. You are one of the last people I'd want to see go through this, but I have to do my job and I am hoping that you will not only understand that, but also respect that."

Josh slid back in his chair, staring at the chief. He then looked down at his hands for a minute. He felt overwhelmed as he considered the chief's comments and the reasons for the chief's question as to his whereabouts prior to going to Stacy's house. The chief gave him time to consider the question.

Then Josh slowly answered, "I left my house around seven o'clock. Had to go to the hardware store to pick up some supplies. I ran into Gordon Emerson while there and I asked his advice on a project I've got coming up. After picking his brain for a while, I headed over to the work site at Stacy's. Got there right at eight o'clock. In addition to Gordon, I talked with a few other people while at the hardware store. I'm sure that any one of them, or all of them if need be, can confirm my presence at that time. Also, I think the hardware store has a security camera that should be able to prove my presence there."

The chief thought for a minute and then said, "That won't be necessary. Thanks for taking the time to answer my question. You can go now, if you'd like."

Josh quipped, "So, I'm not on your suspect list."

The chief calmly replied, "Josh, these questions weren't ever intended to get you onto the suspect list. They were to keep you off the list. Thanks for helping me do that."

Josh thought for a minute, and then got up to leave. When he reached the door, he turned and said, "I've been through a lot the last two days. I found the dead body of a person who was murdered, a person I've known since childhood. My best friend and only employee is sitting in a jail cell. I've just had to explain my whereabouts on the morning of a murder. I do respect the fact that you have a job to do. I apologize if I came across as being disrespectful. That was not my intention."

The chief smiled and said, "No need to apologize, Josh. I've dealt with many disrespectful people in my day. You don't even come close. You are not disrespectful. You are a very good man."

Josh replied, "Well, I don't know about that. But thanks. One last thing, if I may?"

"Sure," the chief said.

Josh said, "Steve told me that he's not worried about his situation. He said the reason he is not worried is because he knows that you will catch the murderer and when you do, you will have to let him out."

The chief leaned back in his chair and said, "Well, we're working on it Josh. We're doing everything we can."

Josh chuckled and said, "Yep. I just experienced that!"

The chief smiled and said, "Thanks Josh, Now, get on home to your wife."

Josh turned and walked out the door.

Chapter Fourteen: Home Sweet Home

Simultaneous to the chief's interview with Josh, Aaron had driven over to Josh's house to interview Andrea.

Andrea was sitting at her computer, doing some freelance graphic design work when Aaron arrived.

Aaron knocked on the door and Andrea answered. She quickly said, "Hi Aaron. Did you find Josh at the work site? He isn't home yet."

Aaron said, "Yes I did. I just wanted to ask you a quick question."

"Oh, sure," Andrea replied, "Come on in."

The children, Caleb and Jacob, were playing when Aaron walked in. Caleb immediately jumped up and ran over to Aaron.

"Is that a real gun?" Caleb asked, staring at the weapon in Aaron's holster, "Did you ever shot somebody with it?"

"Caleb!" Andrea chastised.

Aaron smiled as he said to Andrea, "It's okay." To Caleb, he said, "Yes that is a real gun. No, I've never shot anyone. I hope I never have to."

By then, Jacob had joined his older brother. Caleb continued, "Can I hold your gun?"

"Sorry, no," Aaron said, still smiling. "We are not allowed to take it out of the holster unless we intend to use it. Unless, of course, we are cleaning it or putting it away."

"Oh," replied Caleb. Then he said, "Can I see your badge?"

Aaron chuckled and said, "Sure. But I can't take it off." He then knelt down so that Caleb could see it. Caleb reached out and touched it and said, "Wow." Jacob then immediately reached out so he could touch it, too.

"That's enough," Andrea said, "Tell Officer Aaron 'thank you' and then you two go down to your room and play." The boys begged to stay so they could talk to the policeman. Andrea gave them the stern look that mothers often do and the kids knew they had better do what she said.

"Bye minster policeman, thank you," Caleb said. "Bye, tank you," Jacob added. They then went to their room to play.

"I'm sorry," Andrea said to Aaron, "Please have a seat."

Aaron said, "It's not a problem at all. Cute kids!" He then took a seat on the couch in the front room. Andrea sat in the chair, opposite the couch. She asked, "Can I get you a glass of tea?"

"Oh, no thanks. I'll only be a minute or two," Aaron replied.

Then he continued, "We are trying to establish a time line as best we can to help determine the time of death for Stacy. For the sake of accuracy, we double check whenever we can. The chief is asking Josh the same questions. What time did Josh leave yesterday morning?"

Andrea thought for just a minute and said, "Just before seven o'clock."

Aaron wrote that down and then said, "And how long do you suppose it takes to drive to Stacy's from here?"

Andrea thought for a minute said, "Probably no more than ten to twelve minutes."

Aaron began to write that down when Andrea said, "But, he wasn't going straight over to Stacy's house."

"What do you mean?" Aaron questioned.

Andrea explained, "He had to stop by the hardware store to pick up some things for the project. I think he said paint, nails, sandpaper. Stuff like that."

"Oh, I see," Aaron said, "Do you know if he went straight to Stacy's house from the hardware store?"

"I assume so," Andrea replied.

He thought for a minute and then looked at Andrea, "Do you keep his receipts when he does all this?"

Andrea quickly replied, "We work on his books together. But he always puts his receipts on a shelf above the desk." Andrea had a quizzical look and then said, "Aaron, is there something you aren't telling me? A receipt? Proof that he was at the hardware store? In fact, receipts have a time stamped on them. So, from the receipt, you can tell when he went through the checkout at the hardware store. Come on Aaron, what's this all about?"

Aaron sat with a stunned expression, then explained, "Well, um, wow, you could have been a detective. Very impressive."

Andrea replied, "Yeah, whatever. Cut the nonsense. Why does it seem that you are investigating Josh?"

Aaron took a deep breath, let it out slowly then said, "Andrea, I don't know how to tell you this. But we've had to add Josh to our list of suspects."

Andrea stared at Aaron and then burst out laughing. This was not the reaction he had expected. He argued, "Andrea, this is not a joke. I'm serious. Josh is a suspect."

She laughed even harder. Then she said, "Oh Aaron, that's what makes this so funny. You obviously don't know Josh. He isn't capable of murdering anyone. I have no doubt whatsoever that you guys are wasting your time if you are looking at Josh for this. Wasting-your-time!"

Aaron, tried to explain, "First of all, this is no laughing matter. We take our job seriously and nothing is more series than murder. Second, you never know someone as well as you think you do. No one else was there when Josh found the body. We have every right, in fact, we have every responsibility to consider Josh a suspect until proven otherwise."

Andrea looked at Aaron with intense eyes and then said sternly, "You are absolutely right, OFFICER, this is not a joke. Yours is a very serious job, a critical job, and you'd be much better at it if you didn't waste another minute trying to figure out how many nails Josh bought at the hardware store or whatever your next ridiculous question about my husband might be. YOU may not know Josh as well as you think you do, but I certainly do! You tell that Chief Earl that if word gets out that you two consider Josh to be a suspect, it won't be Josh's reputation that is ruined, it will be your two. You two will look like two incompetent, bumbling fools! Stacy deserves better than this! Now, unless you have any other ludicrous questions for me, please get out of my living room and put your time to better use trying to find the person who murdered Stacy!"

Aaron, feeling like he was back in grade school and had just been chastised by the principal, slowly stood and said, "Um, we're just trying to be thorough in our job. Thank you for your time. I'm sure once the chief finishes talking to Josh, he'll be on his way home."

Andrea smiled and said, "I have no doubt whatsoever that Josh will be home for dinner."

Aaron nodded his head and said, "Ah, yeah. Good afternoon, Andrea." and then he quickly left the house.

After Josh left the chief's office, Dani quickly barged in. She hurriedly said, "I strongly believe that we need to add Dotty to the suspect list."

The chief simply replied, "Continue."

"During the course of the interview it came up that Dotty used to date Shane. In fact, Shane broke up with Dotty so that he could date Stacy," Dani explained, "While talking, she said that Stacy didn't love Shane the way she loves Shane. She then quickly corrected herself and said, 'loved.' It seemed obvious to me that first of all, Dotty still has very strong feelings for Shane, and secondly, she still has unresolved anger issues toward Stacy for stealing Shane from her."

The chief pondered what she had said and then replied, "Well, that certainly is curious. But, honestly, it sounds like a bunch of high school dating drama. Who's going out with who, who likes who, who doesn't like who ..."

Before he could say anything else, Dani continued, "There's more! Dotty and Shane have recently started seeing each other!"

The chief shrugged his shoulders and said, "So. They're both single. It's kind of weird considering their relationship with Stacy, but there's nothing illegal about it. It's still a quantum leap from that to murder."

Dani said, "Yes but, Stacy let Dotty know that she was going to see if she and Shane had any chance of getting back together. That would be the very same Stacy who stole the very same Shane away from Dotty back in their high school days! How's that for motive?!"

The chief leaned forward and said, "It's starting to get very interesting, but do you have anything more? Is there anything that could give us a reason to bring her in for further questioning? You've got a possible motive. What about opportunity?"

Dani, eyes wide open and grinning from ear to ear, said, "How's this for opportunity: Guess who lives directly behind Stacy?"

"You're kidding?" the chief stated.

"You guessed it. Dotty lives behind Stacy. AND, there is a gate which connects their back yards! How bizarre is that?"

"Well, that certainly changes the picture," the chief said. "A gate?! I do not remember seeing a gate along the back of the yard. There was a chain link fence and a large hedge. Are you sure about the gate?"

Dani simply replied, "That's what she said, a gate between her yard and Stacy's."

"Great work, Dani," the chief replied. "Grab the Crime Investigation Kit and let's go over and take a look."

But as the chief stood to leave, Eric came into the office. "Chief," he quickly said, "We've got to let Steve go."

"And why is that?" the chief demanded.

"You told me to work on a time line. Well, according to the time line, Steve could not have committed this crime," Eric explained.

The chief said to Eric, "You're going to have to show it to me. But wait a minute." Then he turned to Dani and said, "Get Aaron and go over to Stacy's. Confirm that there is a gate. If so, there just might be some blood on that gate. With the huge amount of blood we saw around her, whoever stabbed her in the chest could very well have gotten blood on their hands. If so, there would be a good chance of some blood on the gate, if there is a gate and if that is how the person left Stacy's back yard. See if you two can find it, and if so, get a sample so we can do a DNA comparison. That of course can't prove the identity of the suspect, but it would be another piece of the puzzle for us. And, a very big piece at that."

"We're on it, Boss," Dani said as she turned and left.

The chief then sat back down and said to Eric, "Let's talk time line."

Taking a seat, Eric said, "I went back to the neighborhood and knocked on the doors that we didn't get a response from that day, four in all.

The first house there was still no answer. I checked with the neighbor and was informed that the residents of that house have been on vacation all week.

The second house was that of widow Burns. She was visiting her daughter the last four days and just got home this morning. Obviously, she had nothing to contribute to the investigation.

The third house is empty. It's for sale. I looked around to make sure no one had broken in or was hiding out. No one there."

The sheriff impatiently interrupted, "I sure hope this is going somewhere."

Eric continued, "Yes, sir. It is. The fourth house, directly across the street from Stacy's house, is the home of David and Amanda Remington. They left the morning of Stacy's murder to go visit his brother who is very ill. His brother lives about two hours west of here. Came back last night. They said they were shocked to hear the news about Stacy, especially since they had seen her the day they left!"

The chief again interrupted, "Please tell me they know exactly what time they saw Stacy?"

Eric smiled and said, "Indeed they do. They said they left at exactly seven-thirty. They saw her walk down her front walkway to pick up the morning paper. They waved at her as they left! I asked if they were certain. Amanda nodded and said, and I quote, 'David is very meticulous. Whenever we go on any kind of trip, he plans it out in detail, including our time of departure and our E.T.A. We always leave on schedule.' They saw her as they pulled out of their driveway at seven-thirty."

The chief thought out loud, "So, the last time Stacy was seen alive was seven-thirty AM."

Eric said, "Here's what else we know. Doc Clevenger said he leaves his house for his morning walk every morning at seven o'clock. He took a different route than he normally takes, but estimates his conversation with Mrs. Perkins occurred sometime around seven-fifteen. Mrs. Perkins gave the same estimate, which, by the way, still gave her time to drive over to Main Street and create our momentary Main Street Fountain."

"Continue," said the chief.

Eric explained, "Both Dr. Clevenger and Mrs. Perkins said they saw the motorcycle minutes before they met. That puts Steve on the street somewhere around seven-ten or so. Therefore, Steve was long gone at least twenty minutes before Stacy was seen, still alive. He was seen at least twenty minutes before she was murdered."

"She picks up her paper at seven-thirty. Josh arrives at eight o'clock and shortly thereafter finds her body. You've just narrowed the window of her time of death to 30 minutes! Good job Eric," the chief proclaimed. Then he said, "Let's go release Steve."

The chief and Eric approached the cell as Steve lay on the cot. He sat up as the two approached. The chief said, "Steve, do you remember what time you were on Elm yesterday morning?"

Steve said, "Well, I know I was home a little after seven o'clock. I grabbed a quick shower then thought I'd just lay down and close my eyes for about thirty minutes before meeting Josh at eight o'clock, but before I knew it I had slept for two hours. Being up most of the night will do that to you. But to answer your question, I don't know, maybe sometime between seven o'clock and seven-fifteen."

The chief said, "That confirms what our witnesses said. Stacy was killed at least twenty minutes, maybe up to fifty minutes AFTER you drove by. What we have just calculated is that you were at the right place, but at the wrong time."

The chief unlocked the cell door as he spoke. "I'm sorry we kept you here this long, but we could probably have avoided it if you had been a little more cooperative and answered my question."

Steve said, "Yes sir. I know that. But nothing has changed. Still can't answer it. But I know that I'm innocent therefore I knew it was just a matter of time."

The chief nodded and said, "I don't know what you were up to which has caused you to lie to me and your friend, Josh, and which has caused you to be so secretive. I hope for your sake it isn't some kind of illegal activity. I would prefer to not have you in my jail cell ever again. You're free to go."

Steve smiled and said, "Chief Earl, I promise you that I don't ever want to be on the wrong side of these bars again!"

The chief nodded and then he went back to his office.

Eric smiled and slapped Steve on the back as he walked by and said, "See you around."

Steve replied, "Yep, see you around," and walked out the door.

After Steve left, the chief called Eric back into his office. He said, "Good job on the time line. Now, I've got something else for you to take care of."

"Sure thing," Eric said with confidence, feeling very good about himself at the moment.

"I want you to go talk to Mike Lambeau. Find out where he was yesterday morning between seven-thirty and eight o'clock," the chief explained.

"Wow, Mike?! I didn't see that one coming," Eric replied.

The chief gave Eric his reasons, as he had earlier explained to Aaron.

Eric nodded and said, "I'm going to enjoy this. I'll leave immediately."

Dani and Aaron arrived at Stacy's house, the yellow police ribbon still intact, and quickly walked around to the back of the yard. They paused by the porch for a moment, and then they found the gate in the far corner.

"From a distance, you can't even tell there's a gate here," Aaron said.

Upon examining the gate, they found a dark, brownish red substance on the latch as well as on the top bar of the gate. Using their kit, they took a sample from each spot and put the samples into small jars and then placed a lid on each jar. They labeled each jar and placed them in the crime investigation kit.

They did not open the gate, nor did they enter into Dotty's yard. They walked back past the porch and looked at the large bloodstain on the patio. Aaron asked if they were supposed to get a sample from that, as well.

Dani shook her head and said, "No. There's no need to. We all saw Stacy laying right there. They already got a sample from her at the morgue."

They then walked back around to the front yard, ducked under the yellow tape, got into the squad car and returned to the station.

Meanwhile, Chief Earl made a phone call to a longtime friend at the County Examiners Office, Barb Huff. "Hi Barb, this is Fred," he said when the call was transferred to her office.

Barb cheerily replied, "Hello Fred, great to hear your voice. It's been awhile. How is Diane doing?"

"She's fine, Barb. How's Mic?" the chief asked,

"Ornery as ever," Barb quipped. "You need to get him out fishing again. He's always in a better mood once he's had a few trout on the line."

The chief laughed and said, "That sounds like a plan. In fact, the four of us are overdue for a trip into the mountains for a couple of days of chasing the trout around a lake. I do believe Mic and I owe you and Diane a little payback."

"So you still haven't gotten over the fact that the superior of the genders out fished you men once again!" Barb teased. "We'll gladly defend our crown. Especially if the loser cleans all the fish again."

"Don't remind me," Fred said. "It was bad enough that we had to clean them all, but did you have to catch so many?!"

Barb continued, "When you're good, you're good! What can I say? You must admit, that fish fry is as good as it gets. From the lake straight into the frying pan. Makes my mouth water just thinking about it."

The chief agreed, "It was the perfect end to a great couple of days."

Getting back to business, Bard said, "Now, I know you didn't call me about fishing and I'm guessing it's about that murder down there that I heard about."

"Indeed it is," the chief replied. "Michael Terrace sent you a blood sample by courier earlier today, do you know if your office has received it yet?"

"I have no idea, but I can track it down if he did. Is it from the victim or from a suspect?" she asked.

"Victim," the chief said. "I'm going to send another two samples up first thing in the morning. Any chance you can pull some strings and get us a quick turn around to see if the DNA of the samples we're sending in the morning matches what was sent earlier today?"

"I just happen to know a lady who has a bit of clout around here who could probably get that done for you," Barb replied.

The chief laughed and said, "Could this possibly be the same fishing champion we were recently speaking about?"

"One and the same," Barb said, "One and the same!"

She then added, "Typically it can take several days and in some cases a couple of weeks, depending on workload, priorities, quality of sample, etc. As you know, we run these through a batch at a time. We do have a batch ready to be tested in the morning. I can add yours to it, but we probably won't get your second sample in time."

"What time do you open in the morning?" the chief asked.

"We open at eight AM. But I'm always here at seven-thirty," Barb explained.

"I'll have one of my officer's there at seven-thirty, if that works," the chief responded.

"Works fine. But have the officer come around to the back door, they won't let anyone but staff in the front before eight o'clock. Give him my cell number and have him call me when he arrives. I'll meet him at the back door and let him in. He has to be here before eight AM for me to add the samples to our morning test batch," Barb explained.

"Great! He will absolutely be there before eight. What kind of time frame for results are we looking at then?" the chief asked.

"Best case, if I use my Super-Woman powers of influence, the following day. I'll call you immediately as well as fax you a copy of the results. We'll follow that with a certified letter with more details, in case you need that for court."

"Thanks," the chief replied.

"May I make a suggestion?" Barb asked.

"Absolutely! Please do," The chief responded.

"You are hoping, or perhaps you have ample reason to believe, that the sample
Dr. Terrace sent up will be a match for the samples you are sending. Is that correct?" Barb asked.

249

"Yes. We have reason to believe it will be a match," Fred answered.

"As we both have learned over the years, surprises are a part of our ball game. It's always good to be working on a plan B. With that in mind, may I respectfully make a suggestion?" Barb proposed.

"Please continue," the chief responded.

"How about we take a sample of what you are sending and run it through CODIS. Then, if we are surprised to find that your sample doesn't match the sample already here, we've already got a jump on further research. There's always a chance the perpetrator might be in the database. It's just a time saving step in case we need to fall back to plan B" Barb explained.

"I like it!" the chief exclaimed. "Then, if we already have a match we're good to go. If not, we hit the ground running in a new direction. It would certainly surprise me if we got a hit on CODIS, but, one never knows."

Barb summarized, "We'll run DNA comparisons on the samples while simultaneously accessing the FBI database for a matching DNA profile."

"Hey Barb, thanks a lot, I appreciate it," the chief said.

"Glad I can help, Fred. Take care," she replied.

The chief hung up the phone and went to check with Michelle to see if Aaron and Dani had returned.

Meanwhile, Josh had arrived home a short time after leaving the chief's station. As he walked in the door, Andrea quipped, "Well, how's the life of crime working out for you? Is my fugitive home for dinner or are you just here to hide out?"

"So, you've heard? You seem to be taking it all in stride," Josh observed.

"Well, hey, it's not every day your husband is dragged into the chief's station and questioned about a murder. That's sure to lift the spirits of any wife!" she continued in her teasing manner.

Then she looked at Josh and said, "It was Aaron who told me. He stopped by and questioned me about your schedule that morning."

"I'm sorry you had to go through that," he said.

She smiled as she said, "No big deal. I was just fixin' to bake you a cake with a hacksaw in the middle so that you could break out of jail tonight."

He shook his head and said, "Very funny, but it might not be a bad idea for Steve. They're still holding him."

"The truth will eventually surface; it always does. Steve will be fine," she assured him.

"That's pretty much what Steve said," Josh replied.

"Why don't you go get cleaned up and spend some time with the boys before dinner," she suggested.

He gave her a quick kiss and said, "That sounds a whole lot better than spending the night in jail."

He then walked out of the room, looking for his two little buddies.

Eric found Mike at his desk when he entered the newspaper office. Mike looked up and said, "Oh, hi, Eric. Any updates on the Stacy case?"

"In fact," Eric replied, "That's why I'm here."

"Great!" Mike enthused. He set aside a file of papers he was working on and picked up a notepad.

"We need to be strictly off the record for a few minutes, Mike. Otherwise, this isn't going to work," Eric began.

"Oh, man. I hate that, Eric. Just tell me what you can and I'll try to squeeze a little bit more out of you. You know how the system works," Mike pleaded.

"Not this time, Mike. I need you to cooperate on this. Just for a few minutes, then we can go on the record," Eric said firmly.

Mike took a long deep breath, set his notepad and pen down and then said, "Fine. We're off the record, for now."

Eric said, "Good. Now, please tell me where you were on the morning of Stacy's murder, before you arrived at the scene?"

Mike sat with his mouth slightly open, flabbergasted. Eric waited. Mike questioned, "Are you asking me what I think you are asking me?"

Eric said, "Look, I know that you are used to asking the questions. Perhaps now you have a little empathy for those on the receiving end of those tough questions. But this shouldn't be that tough of a question to answer. I'm simply asking you to tell me where you were from, let's say, seven o'clock until eight o'clock the morning of Stacy's murder."

Mike shook his head, then said very slowly, "Based upon your question, I assume you have narrowed down the time for Stacy's murder to that hour. Furthermore, you or the chief, for some insane reason, or out of extreme desperation for a suspect, are looking at me as a possible perpetrator of this murder. Is that what this question is all about?"

Eric leaned in toward Mike and said, "Well, I can't help but notice you haven't answered my question."

Mike gestured with both hands in front of him, palms up, "From about seven-twenty until about eight-twenty, I was at

Lisa's Kitchen having breakfast. I had just left the restaurant and had gotten into my car. I started it up, pulled out into the street and then heard on my scanner Michelle's call to you and Dani. I went straight over to Stacy's, in fact, I arrived there right after you did."

Eric said patiently, "Is your scanner connected to your car, or did you carry it into the restaurant?"

"What difference does that make?!" Mike demanded.

Eric explained, "I'm just curious why you didn't hurry over to Main Street about forty-five minutes earlier when Mrs. Perkins backed into the fire hydrant. Or, is that a story you wouldn't cover?"

Mike answered, "My scanner is connected to my car. It's got one of those plugs that goes into a cigarette lighter socket. I also have a scanner in my office. But I don't have one that is portable enough to just carry around. Furthermore, I did an article on the 'Main Street Fountain.' Even had a picture sent to me by one of our subscribers. I interviewed Mrs. Perkins and Fire Chief Patrick for the article."

"I must have missed that article," Eric said, "I'm sure we'll have no problem confirming your presence at Lisa's Kitchen. Thank you for answering my questions."

Mike quickly said, "Are we back on the record, now?"

"Sure," Eric answered.

"Well," Mike proclaimed, "for the record, I think your line of questions for me is a bunch of nonsense!"

Eric replied, "Just doing my job. Kind of like a reporter, asking questions is a big part of the job."

"Well, now that we are back on the record, I have a few questions about the case," Mike said.

Eric stood and replied, "Sorry, Mike. You'll have to direct your questions to the chief. He's the only one authorized to deal with the press."

With that, he turned and walked out the door.

The chief was sitting at his desk when Dani and Aaron walked into his office. "What did you find?" he quickly asked.

"A gate," Aaron replied. "Way over in the far back corner of the yard. With that high hedge along the back fence, you hardly even notice the gate. It leads into the yard of the house behind Stacy's."

"Anything else?" the chief asked.

"We found, what appears to be blood, smudged on the gate. Both on the latch and on the top crossbar of the gate," Dani explained.

"Were you able to get a good sample?" he asked.

Dani said, "I believe so. From both spots."

"Great! Okay, Aaron I want you to take the samples up north to the County Examiners Office first thing in the morning. Leave early enough to get there around seven-thirty. They don't open until eight o'clock, but I'll give you the cell number for Barb Huff. Call her when you get there and she will meet you at the back door. She'll take your samples and add them to the batch that they'll be running through first thing in the morning. It's critical that you get there around seven-thirty so that our samples can be included in that batch! They'll be able to compare the DNA to what was sent from Stacy's blood sample. Assuming they match, I will approach the judge about getting a search warrant for Dotty's house. I don't want to scare her off, so no one approaches Dotty until we get that warrant, understood?"

They both nodded.

The chief added, "Just in case our samples don't match up with Stacy's, Barb is also going to run the DNA samples through CODIS, on the longshot we might get a hit from the FBI database."

"Sorry, boss," Dani said. "I know what CODIS is, but I can't remember what the acronym actually stands for."

Aaron laughed and said, "I didn't want to say anything, but I can't remember that one either. We've got more acronyms around here than a cherry tree has blossoms in the spring!"

The chief smiled as he explained, "Combined DNA Index System. It contains DNA profiles contributed by federal, state and local participating forensic laboratories.

It's managed by the FBI, but is accessible to local law enforcement jurisdictions."

The chief added, "It's a long shot and I doubt we'll get a hit, but as I keep saying, leave no stone unturned. Meanwhile, I'm confident the blood you found on the gate will be a match with Stacy's."

"Sounds good, chief," Aaron replied, while Dani nodded her head in agreement. Aaron then added, "Speaking of evidence and suspects, I noticed the cell is empty. Did you cut Steve loose?"

"Yep," the chief answered. "Eric completed the time line. Stacy was seen in her front yard at seven-thirty that morning. Steve rode his motorcycle up Elm shortly after seven. It no longer matters why he was there, Stacy was still alive after Steve was seen on Elm."

Aaron thought for a minute and said, "That means that if Coach Stewart has anyone confirm that he was in his office, he'd be off the list as well. Right?"

The chief thought for a moment, then replied, "Yes. But let's not get ahead of ourselves. Let's make sure someone can corroborate his story. At this point, I just don't trust him. Until someone can confirm his statement as to his whereabouts, he stays on the list. But, it does remove Richard White from the list. His alibi has been confirmed."

Dani asked, "What about Shane?"

"He's still a secondary suspect. Until some solid evidence surfaces concerning him, we'll leave him alone, for now," the chief explained.

"Sounds good, chief," Aaron said, as he and Dani turned and walked out of the chief's office.

As Josh was sitting down with his family, there was a knock on the door. Andrea teased, "Looks like the chief tracked you down, want me to get busy preparing that cake?"

As he stood to go to the door Josh shot back, "Sure, and see if you can fit a jackhammer in it as well."

When he opened the door he was surprised to see Steve standing there, grinning from ear to ear.

Steve, with arms stretched wide, said, "I told you, it was just a matter of time!"

Josh gave him a big hug and said, "Get in here you knucklehead."

Andrea rounded the corner and said, "Well, what do we have here, two convicts standing right in my living room. I do declare!"

She then gave Steve a hug and a kiss on the cheek. She then said, "We're just getting ready to eat, please join us."

"You don't have to ask me twice. I'm starved!" Steve exclaimed.

The boys loved their "uncle" Steve and wanted to run over and climb onto his lap as he sat down at the dinner table. Andrea quickly sent them back to their seats to finish their dinner.

Over dinner Steve explained that the chief had released him based upon the time line that Eric had drawn up. "The truth was in the time line," he said.

"And the truth shall set you free," Andrea proclaimed.

"I guess now I don't have to go visit you in the cell at eight o'clock tomorrow morning," Josh said, happily.

Eric responded, "My temporary residence at the police station is over, for good!"

"Let's hope so," Andrea chimed in.

When the main course was concluded, Andrea asked if they were ready for dessert. The boys quickly responded that they wanted dessert but Andrea informed them that they had to finish their dinner, first. She then again asked Steve if he'd like some.

Steve said, "Absolutely. What are we having?"

Josh looked at Andrea, they both smiled and together they said, "Cake!"

Chapter Fifteen: A Warrant

The next day was business as usual in the police station. Michelle came into the station promptly at 8:00. She saw Dani and Eric sitting at their desks and the chief in his office, but didn't see Aaron.

She asked Eric, "Is Aaron on patrol this morning or is he off today?"

Before Eric could answer, Dani chimed in, never wanting to miss a chance to poke some fun at Eric, "Michelle, you're wasting your time asking Eric any questions at eight AM. Only one of his two brain cells are working at this hour."

Eric responded, "And Officer Gilbert is still applying her makeup, and we certainly don't want that to be interrupted!"

Michelle just shook her head and said, "Wow, you two are at it early today. Are you sure that you aren't brother and sister, because you sure act like it?!"

Dani quickly replied, "If he were my younger brother, I would have drowned him when we were kids."

To which Eric smiled and said, "If I were your younger brother, I would have drowned myself!" Dani couldn't help but laugh at that retort.

Michelle then said, "Would one of you please just answer my question? Where's Aaron?"

Dani explained that Aaron had made the drive up north to the County Examiner's Office to deliver the blood samples for DNA analysis and that he should be on his way back to Springerville soon. "He should be back mid-morning," she said.

Eric and a sheriff's deputy had been handling most of the calls, the others filling in as needed. These included a stolen bicycle, a minor fender-bender caused by a teenager trying to parallel park for the first time, a shoplifting incident at the local drugstore, a possible break-in (turned out that the older gentleman had simply forgotten to close his front door when he went to the store.

When he arrived home, he saw the door open and thought he was being burglarized), traffic control at a small brush fire, a domestic abuse accusation (on which Eric took Dani along to the scene, as was their protocol) a report of an abandoned vehicle, a report of a gun being shot from someone's backyard which turned out to be a young teen shooting a BB gun at some sparrows (all three officers responded to that call,) as well as a few other miscellaneous calls.

When Aaron returned to the station, he called the school to set up an appointment with Coach Stewart. The coach informed him that he had a break in about twenty minutes if Aaron could get over there in time. If not, he'd have to wait until the next day. Aaron let the coach know that we would indeed be there in twenty minutes.

When Aaron arrived at the coach's office, he glanced over to see if the Spirit Spear was still in the corner. It was.

Coach Stewart said, "Better make this quick, I've only got a short break."

"No problem," Aaron replied. "Let's get right to it."

"Yes, let's do," the coach shot back.

Aaron began, "Yesterday you said you were here in your office at 6:30 the previous morning. Is that correct?"

"That's what I said, because that's where I was," the coach answered.

"Was there anyone else here with you?" Aaron asked.

The coach chuckled as he said, "What's the problem, kid, don't trust me? I said I was here. I have no reason to lie."

"Just doing my job, coach. Routine question. Was there anyone else here with you?" Aaron repeated.

"In fact, there was. Shane was sitting right where you are. We were discussing which plays would work best for the upcoming opponent and we worked on that until time for classes. Our meeting started at six-thirty. Call Shane, he'll confirm it. A few other coaches saw us here, check with them. The janitor is always here early, ask him. And if none of that satisfies you, check the school security cameras. Because it's obvious you'd never believe me. As I told you yesterday, I wouldn't go anywhere near that girl."

Aaron decided that he had all of the information that he was going to get and that it was best to walk away from what was quickly becoming another tense situation. So, he stood and looked down at the coach and said, "Stacy. Her name is Stacy. That girl that you keep referring to has a name. The one who was murdered. The one Shane loved and married. The one who leaves two little children and two grieving parents behind. Her-name-is-Stacy." Then he turned and walked out of the door.

As Aaron was leaving the coaches office, he saw the old janitor, Bruce Ford, walking away from the building. Aaron quickly caught up with Bruce and introduced himself. He asked the janitor about the morning in question, if he remembers seeing Coach Stewart in his office, and if so, at what time. Bruce thought for a minute and then replied that yes, he did remember seeing the coach there. He had walked by the office at about 6:45 and had seen the coach as well as Coach Pruitt in Coach Stewart's office. Aaron thanked Bruce and then turned to leave.

But, Aaron didn't leave the school, not just yet. He went directly to the front office and asked to see Principal Pace. Randy Pace came out of his office and shook Aaron's hand, he smiled and led Aaron into his office.

Aaron said, "Sorry to barge in on you like this, but I need your help."

"No problem at all. How can I help?" Randy said.

Aaron asked, "Do you have security cameras on campus?"

"Yes we do," Randy explained, "They are state-of-the-art cameras and they are strategically located at several locations around campus."

Aaron continued. "Do you have one that views the entrance to the coaches' offices?"

"We have a camera pointed at each of the entrances to every building on campus," Randy stated.

Aaron asked, "May I view the video from the morning of Stacy's death, the video that would show who all entered the coaches' offices before school started?"

"I'm assuming this has something to do with a suspect in Stacy's murder?" the principal asked.

"Perhaps," Aaron answered, "But let's not get ahead of ourselves. We simply need to confirm the whereabouts of certain individuals at certain times. All part of the process of investigation. I will trust you to keep this confidential."

"I understand," the principal said, "Tim Reese heads up our I.T. department. The video resources are in his office."

The two walked down the hall to Tim's office and the principal introduced Tim to Aaron and explained what they needed. He also stressed the importance of confidentiality. Tim, turning to the recently installed Aspen Monitoring System, was able to quickly access the video in question. It showed Coach Stewart walking into the building at 6:13. Two other coaches walked in at 6:24. Shane trotted up to the door at 6:31, and entered into the building.

Aaron asked if Tim could make him a copy of what they had just watched. Tim assured him that he could, and Aaron provided him with the email address to send it to.

Aaron thanked the principal and Tim and then returned to his station.

When Aaron arrived back at the station, he went in to report to the chief about his conversation with Coach Stewart.

Aaron said to the chief, "Looks like the coach has a solid alibi for his whereabouts from six-thirty on, the morning of Stacy's death. I've reviewed security camera footage and there are witnesses that confirmed that he and Shane were at the school. I honestly believe, however, that in a rage he could do it. It all gets down to a timing issue," Aaron explained.

"I agree," the chief replied. "However, his dislike of her does not constitute evidence. If he has witnesses for his whereabouts at the time of her death, then that takes him off the list. Eric's timeline closes the door on the coach as a suspect."

"Furthermore," Aaron quickly added, "Shane wasn't high on my suspect list anyway, but we now know exactly where he was from six-thirty on into the day."

"Strike those two from the list," the chief said, and then added, "Good job, Aaron."

As the afternoon drug on, there were the usual volumes of reports to be written and filed. The day did not pass quickly enough for Chief Earl. He was relieved when it was finally time to go home.

The chief arrived at his station at 7:00 the next morning. Even though it would probably be later in the day before he got the DNA results, he was anxious for the report to come in. He tried to busy himself by catching up with some paper work, but couldn't help but look at the clock every ten minutes.

Dani arrived at 7:30. "We should get those DNA results today, right?" she asked the chief.

"If all goes well, yes," he answered as nonchalantly as he could.

"Is Mrs. Huff going to call you once she gets the results?" she asked, not caring if the chief knew that she was anxious about the results and moving forward accordingly.

"Well, yes. I guess so. We'll see," he calmly replied.

"What time do you think she'll call?" Dani asked.

"Don't know," the chief said without looking up from his work.

"How long do you think it will take?" she pressed.

The chief let out a long sigh, looked up at Dani and asked sternly, "Officer, don't you have some work to do?"

"Yes sir," she said, as she turned and went back to her desk.

Michelle arrived at 8:00 and as she walked toward her desk, she said as she passed Dani's desk, "I can't wait to hear what the DNA results are."

"Yeah," Dani whispered, "just don't say anything about it around the chief."

Michelle laughed and whispered back, "He doesn't like to show any excitement or anxiety about things. So he hides it by getting grumpy."

"No kidding," Dani replied.

Michelle sat down at her desk and started working.

Twenty minutes later, the chief called Michelle into his office.

He said, "I've been on the phone with County Attorney, Mark Prescott getting his input on a warrant. I'm keeping him apprised of the situation and getting his advice on some of the legal aspects of things. Call Judge Hardman's office and see if he's in. I don't want to talk to him on the phone; I want to walk over to his office if he has any time this morning."

Michelle went to her desk and returned a few minutes later, "Christy said that the Judge is in and he doesn't have a case until ten o'clock. She said you can drop in any time before then."

"Thanks," the chief said, as he immediately stood to leave.

As he passed the desks of Dani and Eric he explained, "I'm going to go visit the judge and see if I can grease the skids a bit in regards to a search warrant."

"Sounds good," Eric said as the chief walked out.

Dani looked at Eric and said, "Of course, that means I'm in charge until he gets back in the office."

Eric laughed and said, "Keep dreaming!"

Dani continued, "Hey, seniority. It's all about seniority."

Eric replied, "Lucky for you it's not about competency."

Dani, trying not to laugh, said, "Ha-ha, very funny. Speaking of competency, why don't you go out there and wash my squad car? That's the one thing you are fairly competent at."

Eric rolled his eyes and said, "That'll happen about the same time you start doing my laundry every week."

Without looking up from her work, Dani said, "Now who's dreaming?"

Michelle, sitting at her desk and listening to the banter, just shook her head and thought to herself, "Predictable. So predictable."

Judge Philip Hardman had been a Judge in Springerville just a few years longer than Frederick Earl had been chief of police. Sixty-four years old, heavy set, graying hair and huge bushy gray eyebrows gave him a no-nonsense appearance which was consistent with his character. He would tolerate no shenanigans in his court and gave very little latitude to attorneys when they questioned witnesses. An attorney had better be prepared when he walked into Judge Hardman's court, or he would quickly regret that he was unprepared.

The judge's aid, Christy, showed the chief into the judges office when he arrived.

"Good morning, Fred," Judge Hardman said as the chief entered, "How's that murder investigation coming along?"

"Good morning, Judge," the chief said as he sat, "That's exactly why I'm here."

He then explained the situation with the gate between the yards, past and present relationships between Dotty, Shane and Stacy, and the reason they now consider Dotty to be a suspect. He added the details about the DNA and that he expected a match.

The judge thought for a moment and then said, "Thus far, it's very flimsy evidence. Anybody could have used that gate."

"That's exactly why we need a search warrant," the chief said.

"Yes, I get that," the judge said as he continued to ponder the situation. He then added, "Furthermore, getting a warrant does not guarantee that you will find any evidence on the premises."

"Of course," the chief said, "if no evidence is found connecting Dotty to the crime scene, we will then remove her from the suspect list. However, if there is evidence, we can proceed accordingly. But, we need a warrant to determine that."

"Okay, I will opine that the DNA match would provide the grounds for that warrant," the judge answered.

"We'd like to move on it as quickly as possible," the chief said, "If any evidence hasn't already been destroyed or discarded, we'd like to find it while it's still there."

"Fair enough," the judge said, "I'm in court at ten o'clock, will you have your results by then?"

"I doubt it," the chief replied.

The judge said, "We'll break for lunch for about 90 minutes. Then we'll spend the better part of the afternoon back in court. Christy will know where to reach me if you get your confirmation during that break. Meanwhile, I can have her draft the search warrant. But you're going to have to tell me what you'd like the warrant to cover."

He then called Christy into his office and explained to her about the warrant. She then took notes while the chief began, "We want to look for any weapons or anything that can be used for a weapon."

"Stop there," the judge interrupted. "'Anything that can be used as a weapon' is far too broad. I can't give you that much latitude. Weapons is one thing, but you have to be more specific on the rest."

The chief said, "Okay. How about weapons, including any sharp pointed object that could be used as a knife, or clever, or spear, or hatchet, or similar weapon."

The judge thought for a minute and replied, "Since you have tied the word 'similar' into knife, clever, spear or hatchet, I can give you that. What else?"

"Any clothing which have blood stains on them, including but not limited to, shoes or gloves," the chief added.

"No problem, what else?" the judge asked.

The chief continued, "Any correspondence including letters, post cards, notes, etc. Also, including methods of correspondence such as computers and any electronic communication devices which might reveal an ongoing argument or any threats between the suspect and the victim."

The judge said, "The verbiage is a little rough, but its boilerplate stuff. Christy can smooth it out and make sure it holds water."

Christy nodded her head as she continued to write.

The chief added, "We'd like to include the house, the garage, any storage sheds or tool sheds, and any exterior closets or cabinets such as on a porch, patio, carport, etc."

"Done, but of course, limited to such places on that particular property," the judge said.

"I understand. Thanks. I appreciate it," the chief responded.

"Christy will have it drafted and ready for me to sign. But remember, this is all contingent upon you getting the DNA match you are anticipating," the judge concluded.

"Understood," the chief said.

The two men stood and shook hands; Christy showed the chief to the door and he walked back to his office.

When he returned to his office, the first thing he did was to ask Michelle if the County Examiner's Office had called.

When she told him that they had not, he walked into his office and continued to wait.

The morning passed without a call about the DNA results. At 12:15, the chief and all three officers were still at their desks. Michelle asked the chief if he was going to lunch.

"No," he answered abruptly, "Not hungry."

She asked the other three and Aaron said, "Think I'll just hang out here in case we have to move quickly once that phone call comes in."

Eric said, "Same here."

Dani nodded her agreement.

Michelle said, "How about I get a pizza, a couple of salads and some drinks from Kennelli's?"

"Sounds good," Aaron and Eric enthusiastically chimed.

"I'll go with you to help carry, since apparently there are no gentlemen here to do so," Dani quipped.

Aaron started to offer to help but Eric said, "Just ignore her. Besides that, she needs the exercise."

As Dani got up from her desk, she just happened to pass by Eric's desk and "accidently" happened to knock over a small cup holding his paper clips.

Eric said, "You are SO mature."

Aaron laughed and said, "Two peas in a pod."

Michelle shook her head and said, "Some things never change. I'll call in the lunch order."

Kennelli's was an Italian restaurant, even though its owner, Ken Murphy was Irish. The restaurant was decorated with a variety of photos of iconic Italian landmarks, such as the Colosseum in Rome, the Trevi Fountain, Saint Peter's Basilica in the Vatican, the Pantheon, the leaning tower of Pisa, the streets of Pompeii, the Grand Canal in Venice, the Statue of David, the Sistine Chapel, brightly colored homes on the cliffs of the Amalfi Coast, and several more. Of course, small green, white and red Italian flags were scattered throughout the restaurant.

Ken had hired many a high school student over the years and considered their employment as an opportunity to teach business skills, good customer service and an all-around healthy work ethic. Many a Springerville teen had their first employment at Kennelli's. Located right on Main Street, near the courthouse, it was a popular establishment for teens and adults alike as many Main Street business men and women enjoyed their fare.

Michelle had ordered two large pizzas, the meat lover's special and the other with white cheese, tomatoes, garlic and olive oil. She also ordered two large salads, which she figured could be shared. She knew the soft drinks of preference for everyone at the station, and these, too, were ordered.

As Ken usually did, he offered a special discount for law enforcement.

Michelle, as usual, politely declined the generous offer. "You know Chief Earl's rules," she said, "No police discounts are to be accepted by anyone in his department.

He doesn't even want to give the hint of an appearance of showing favoritism based upon any such gift."

Ken smiled and nodded and said, "He's a stickler for the rules, isn't he?" Michelle said simply, "Absolutely."

Ken said, "Just one of the many reasons for his stellar reputation." He added, "You know, we can deliver these any time you'd like."

Michelle smiled and said, "Sometimes it's nice to get out of the office for a little walk."

Ken nodded and said, "Yes indeed." Then Michelle and Dani carried their meal back to the station.

They set the pizza and salads in the conference room and Michelle got some paper plates, napkins and plastic ware. She took a big slice of the meat lover's special into the chief's office even though he had said he wasn't hungry. She placed it and a glass of diet coke on his desk, without saying anything.

He looked up from his computer and said, "Oh, ah, thanks."

"You are welcome," she said as she walked out of the office.

Meanwhile, Aaron grabbed a couple of slices of the meat lover's special, Eric grabbed a slice from each pizza. Aaron also took a salad.

Dani took a slice of the white cheese pizza and some salad. When no one was looking, she went back for a second slice.

Michelle took a very thin slice of the white cheese pizza and some salad.

Eric went back for two more slices of the meat lover's special, not caring who saw. As he walked back to his desk, Dani started making some cow, mooing sounds.

Aaron laughed as he went back for a slice of the white cheese.

Dani asked Aaron if they had heard anything while she and Michelle were gone.

"Not a word," Aaron replied.

Meanwhile, at the salon, Dotty went about her business as usual. Cheerfully greeting her customers and conversing with them and others in her salon. She had spent the last two evenings at home looking for locations for her next vacation. She had always wanted to go to the Bahamas or the Caribbean, as well as certain locations in Mexico. She knew a little about some of the islands in the Caribbean, but had not realized there were so many and spent most of one evening reading about each island. Just out of curiosity, she also looked at a variety of Canadian destinations. While she would love to have visited any of the countries in Europe, she figured that such a trip was well beyond her budget.

On this particular morning, while Chief Earl arrived at his office at 7:00, Dotty arrived at her salon at 7:30. While the chief was eating his meat lover's pizza for lunch, Dotty ate a granola bar, a few slices of cheese and some carrot and celery sticks she had brought from home. While the chief's staff was finishing up reports and waiting for a phone call from the County Examiner's Office, Dotty's staff was cutting hair, coloring hair, and chatting with customers.

Over lunch Dotty decided to look at Brazil as another possibility for a vacation trip. The photos of the beaches were beautiful. She added Rio de Janeiro to her list. She then did a google search concerning hair salons, help wanted, in Rio. She spent the next hour reading about Rio, checking apartment prices, reading the job opportunities, and looking at pictures of the city and the surrounding area. She then made a decision. She called Brittany into her office. After Brittany entered, Dotty asked her to close the door and take a seat.

"I'm thinking of taking some time off. I'm hoping you can run things here while I'm gone," Dotty explained.

Brittany had run the salon on several occasions before, so it was no big deal to her that Dotty would make such a request. She smiled and said, "Sure thing! Where are you going?"

Dotty thought for a minute and then said, "I'm thinking of spending a week or two up in Canada."

"Wow!" Brittany exclaimed, "It'll be awfully cold up there right now."

"Yes. I know. But I feel like doing some skiing, riding a snowmobile, sitting by a nice warm fire and doing some reading. I just want to get away for a little bit," Dotty explained.

"Sounds good," Brittany responded. "When are you thinking of going?"

"As soon as possible," Dotty replied. "Very spur of the moment, but, I know you can handle things here, so, why wait! I might even leave in the next day or two. I'll let you know as soon as I get some travel details worked out."

"Oh my gosh!" Brittany said with a shocked expression. "That IS quick! How long do you think you'll be gone?"

"Probably just a week or so," Dotty shrugged. "I just need a break."

Brittany enthusiastically replied, "I understand. Don't you worry about anything here. We'll hold down the fort while you're gone. You've worked very hard and you deserve to enjoy some time to yourself. We've got you covered!"

"Thanks," Dotty smiled as she responded to Brittany's statement.

After Brittany left her office, Dotty got on her computer and looked up flights to Rio de Janeiro. She looked at round trip flights leaving the next day and returning in two weeks. She then looked at one-way flights. She found one leaving the next afternoon and booked a one-way flight to Rio. She then looked at several hotels near the airport and made a reservation at one. Next, she started looking at apartments for rent.

The phone call came in at 2:45.
Michelle came to the chief's door and said, "I have Mrs. Huff on line 2."

The chief didn't say a word to Michelle, but quickly picked up his phone and hit the button for line 2. "Hi, Barb," he said quickly.

Barb replied, "Hello Fred, they just concluded running your samples and the test results have been dropped off on my desk. It's a match. Of course, the sample that came from the coroner's office was an unblemished, premier sample, Dr. Michael Terrace always does good work. The second pair of samples had a few contaminants which had to be filtered out, but other than that, they are also a good pair of samples. The test results are solid; all three samples come from the same person."

"That's what I expected. It's amazing that you could turn this around so quickly. I owe you big time! Can you send a preliminary report via fax?" the chief asked.

"It's being prepared as we talk. You should have it in about 15 minutes," she explained.

"Thanks Barb," the chief said enthusiastically.

"Glad I could help. Now, do what you do best, go out and catch the bad guy," Barb encouraged.

The chief replied, "Well, this may surprise you, but this particular suspect is a bad gal."

"That is a surprise. It's not very often you hear of a female murderer. I'm sure there is a lot more to that story, which neither of us have time for right now," she responded.

"Indeed. I'll give you the entire story when we're on that next fishing trip," the chief said.

"I'm looking forward to it. Talk to you later," Barb concluded.

"Thanks again. Bye," the chief said as he hung up the phone.

The chief then called everyone into his office. Once they were assembled he said, "The DNA test is a match. Stacy's blood was on the gate between her house and Dotty's house. Of course, that in itself doesn't prove anything, other than whoever killed Stacy used that gate. However, based on Dotty's conversation with Dani, along with the DNA match, the judge has opined that we have reasonable cause to get a search warrant of her house."

The chief continued, "Michelle, we should be getting a fax in about fifteen minutes with the preliminary report from the DNA tests. Run a few copies and then give me a copy to take over to the judge. The search warrant is all set, all he has to do is sign it. Let's just hope he isn't in court the rest of the day. Dani, you and I need to discuss how we approach Dotty about the search warrant while she is still at her salon."

Dani asked, "Why not just wait until she goes home after work and serve it right then?"

The chief explained, "We have no idea what time she will go home. She might be working late, she might stop at the grocery store, she might meet someone for drinks or dinner. I don't want us waiting into the evening to serve the warrant. It's going to take some time to search the house. I don't want to go late into the night, if we can avoid it. We'll start as soon as we can. But we have to get the judge to sign the warrant, which means waiting until he is out of court, or at least until he takes a break."

The chief continued, "When we get there, of course, everyone wears gloves. I'll stay with Dotty in the living room. Dani, you take the bedroom. You'll be looking for any clothes that have blood on them. Check the floor of the closet, the hamper, under the bed, behind doors, all of the drawers, check everywhere. Locate the washer and dryer and make sure there are no clothes in either of them. You are looking for blouse, pants, shoes, gloves, any clothing with blood on it. While doing that, keep your eyes open for any weapon.

Aaron, you and Eric start in the kitchen and then check the garage. Your primary focus is a weapon. Of course, if you see any blood on any clothes, bag it. Oh, also check all trash cans, inside and out, for clothes, gloves or a weapon. The weapon probably isn't your typical steak knife. The coroner said it was almost like a spear. Look for anything sharp and approximately two inches wide at its widest point. Also, long enough to penetrate deep enough to reach the area of the heart."

Eric asked, "Chief, Dotty is a tiny little gal. Is she really strong enough to make such a wound? I mean, could she even have stabbed with something, whatever it was, that deep into Stacy's chest?"

"Although women only commit about ten percent of the murders in America, knives are the second most common method used by them, accounting for about twenty-three percent of those murders. In a fit of rage, you'll be amazed what people can do," the chief explained. "Years of pent up frustration and anger all comes pouring out in one violent thrust, plus hitting her chest at just the right location at just the right angle, absolutely she could have done it," the chief said.

He quickly added, "But that's the prosecutor's job to prove it. We just need to get him good, solid, legal evidence so that he can do his job. So, let's make sure we do this right today."

They all nodded.

He said, "One final thing. After you've completed those searches, look for any kind of correspondence between the two. Check trash cans, desks, counter tops for letters, notes, cards, etc. We'll take any computers and electronic communication devices and turn all of that over to the County Attorney's office to scrutinize."

Again, they all nodded.

The chief concluded, "Michelle, call over to the judges office and give Christy a heads up. See if she has any idea when the judge might be available to sign the warrant. And let me know the second that fax comes in."

"Will do," she said as she left.

He turned to Dani and said, "Let's discuss how you will approach Dotty at her salon."

They then discussed different scenarios Dani might face and how she was to respond in each situation. Aaron and Eric would be in a patrol car down the block from the salon, but with a clear line of sight of the front door of the salon, in case Dani ran into any problems, which was not likely, but the chief was taking no chances. Once they had Dotty in Dani's car, Aaron was to radio the station to let the chief know, and they would all meet at Dotty's house.

As the meeting broke up at 3:00 and as the chief was walking back to his office, he passed Michelle's desk. She informed him that the judge was in court and Christy did not know what time the court session would end that day, but she had promised to call Michelle the very minute it ended. Everyone went to their desks and waited.

The fax from the County Examiner's office came through at 3:05. Everyone in the office tried to busy themselves with reports, checking emails and text messages, anything to at least look busy. The minutes crept by.

Christy called at 3:40 and said to Michelle, "The judge just adjourned the court session for the day. He is now back in his chambers. Tell Chief Earl he can come over at any time."

Upon hearing this, the chief told Dani to go ahead and pick up Dotty, as they had discussed, and then to take her to her home. Aaron and Eric went in another car and headed out to position themselves just down from Dotty's salon. Meanwhile, the chief walked over to see Judge Hardman and presented him with the DNA report from the County Examiners Office, which Barb Huff had faxed him. The judge looked it over, nodded, and then signed the prepared warrant. The chief, with search warrant in hand, then headed back to the station to await Aaron's call.

Chapter Sixteen: With Friends Like This...

When Dani arrived at the Elite Short Cuts Salon, Dotty was in her office at her computer. When Brittany escorted Dani into the office, Dotty frowned, turned off her computer and said, "Oh, you're back." Brittany closed the door and returned to the front desk.

Dani said, "Yes, I am. I told you that I had some more questions, but I'd like to ask you those questions at your home."

Dotty, with a look of shock, asked, "At my home?! I'm not going home now. I have a four o'clock appointment. You can ask your questions right here in my office, but you have to be finished by four o'clock."

Dani patiently said, "Dotty, you are going to have to cancel that appointment or have someone cover it for you. Chief Earl wants to meet you at your house to ask you a few questions. We need to go there to continue this."

Dotty was stunned. She could feel her heart rate quicken as she fought back some tears. With a quivering voice, she said, "Chief Earl is welcome to come here to talk to me, or perhaps he can make an appointment for tomorrow. I'm available her tomorrow, late in the afternoon. I see no need to meet him at my house."

Although they did not want to immediately mention the search warrant while Dotty was still at the salon, Dani and the chief had discussed at what point Dani might in fact need to do so. She reasoned that she was now at that point. She hoped that if she remained calm, Dotty might also remain calm.

So, as calmly as she could, she said, "Dotty, the chief has a search warrant, issued by the judge, to search your home. He is waiting there now. He would also like to ask you a few questions. I don't think you want him coming here to serve that warrant, nor to ask you questions. I don't think you want to have to explain to your employees and clients why Chief Earl was here and why you then had to leave with him. Out of respect for you, he will meet you at your home where he hopes this can all be resolved without creating a big scene here."

Dotty quickly asked, "Where what can be resolved? What exactly are we trying to resolve?"

Dani explained, "He has some unresolved questions which he would like to ask you himself."

Dotty said, "And what if I don't want to answer any of those questions? What if I don't want to meet him at my house? What if I don't want to meet him at all?!"

Dani, still trying her best to present an air of calmness and reason said, "As Chief of Police, he has the lawful right to detain you for questioning. If you refuse to cooperate, we will have to put you in handcuffs and take you to the police station. He will then present the search warrant there. If you still refuse, he will then have the authority to break down your front door to search your home."

Dotty just stared at Dani.

Dani continued, "Dotty, you don't want to go through all that and you certainly don't want everyone to see you going through all of that. Why don't you just walk out of here with me as peaceful as can be and we'll go to your house and put this all behind us."

Dotty started to cry. Dani gave her a few minutes to compose herself. Dotty then looked at her and said, "He just wants to ask some questions? That's all he wants to do?"

Dani now chose her words very carefully, "The chief wants to ask a couple of simple questions. That's when he will present you with the search warrant. You are Stacy's closest friend. You might have some information about her which can help us find her killer. We need your help. Let's just drive over to your house and take care of this."

Dotty thought for a moment and then said, "Okay. We'll walk out together, but no handcuffs and no holding my arm."

Dani said, "I'm okay with that. We'll do this together."

Dotty then said, "And I'll have to get someone to cover my four o'clock appointment."

Dani said, "Of course."

With that, Dotty stood up and retrieved her purse. She stopped in front of her mirror, dabbed at her eyes, cleared her throat and forced a smile as she walked out of her office. She approached Brittany and asked if she had an opening at 4:00. Brittany said that she already had someone coming in then. Another beautician, Amber, said she was available. Dotty asked her to take care of Mrs. Fowler for her at 4:00. She then told Brittany that she and Dani were going out for a little while and asked Brittany to lock up when everyone was done. The two then walked out as nonchalantly as they could.

Once outside the salon, Dani led Dotty over to her squad car and reached for the back door to let Dotty in. Dotty looked around and said, "Do I have to ride in the back?"

"Sorry, yes," was all Dani said. So, Dotty got in as quickly as possible and Dani closed the door. Dani then got into the driver's seat, fastened her seat belt, and pulled away from the curb.

Unbeknownst to Dotty, Aaron and Eric, in another car about one hundred feet behind them, also pulled out and followed them to Dotty's home.

Eric immediately called the chief on his radio and simply said, "We're on our way."

The chief calmly replied, "Ten-Four." Then, he walked out of his office, got into his squad car and drove over to Dotty's house.

Twelve minutes after leaving the salon, Dani pulled into Dotty's driveway. The chief had just parked in front of the house. Aaron and Eric pulled in behind the chief. Dani got out and opened the door for Dotty, who stepped out and walked quickly to the front door. Dani and the chief followed, farther back Aaron and Eric also made their way up to the door. Dotty found her keys in her purse, unlocked the door and entered the house, leaving the door standing open. The four officers followed her into the house.

Dotty walked across the room and set her purse on the kitchen counter, which separated the family room and the kitchen. She turned and crossed her arms over her chest and said to Dani, "Now what?"

The chief answered, "Dotty, we have a warrant to search your house," as he handed her the warrant.

She took the warrant, glanced at it briefly, set it on the counter and said, "Go ahead."

The chief nodded to the other three, who immediately began following the instructions the chief had given them earlier that day.

The chief asked Dotty to please sit down on the couch and informed her that he would like to ask her a few questions. She let out a long breath, then sat on the couch.

The chief pulled up a chair from the breakfast table and sat directly across from Dotty, a small coffee table between them. The chief asked, "Dotty, where were you on the morning that Stacy was murdered?"

"I was here at my house, then I went to the grocery store. When I heard the terrible news, I went to Stacy's house and then to her parents' house to be with them," Dotty answered.

Dani went into Dotty's bedroom, stopping to put on a pair of latex gloves as she glanced around the room. She first looked behind the door she had just entered. There were no clothes on the floor nor hanging on the back of the door. She walked around the room and quickly looked under the bed, again, no clothes were found. She went into the bathroom and found a robe hanging on the back of the door. She examined it but found no blood stains. She looked around the bathroom and thought, "She's a meticulously clean girl."

Dani then went into the small, walk-in closet. Clothes hung along both sides of the closet, as well as along the back wall. A shoe rack was loaded with a variety of shoes. Additional shoes were neatly lined up under both rows of clothes along the sides of the closet. There were no clothes lying on the floor. A clothes hamper stood at the back of the closet, below a row of blouses and shirts that were hanging below a shelf, a variety of items on top of the shelf.

Dani opened the hamper, which was about two-thirds full. She began to slowly remove the clothing, one article at a time, and examined each item for any blood stains

The chief asked Dotty if she had gone over to see Stacy that morning.

Dotty answered, "No, as I said, I was here at my house, then I went to the grocery store."

Dani had hoped she would find some kind of evidence in the hamper, but as she neared the bottom she started to think that nothing would be found. There were only a few items left when she pulled out a small t-shirt, white, with a red rose on the front. She looked at the front and back of the shirt, seeing no blood stains, she then began to drop the shirt onto the small pile of clothes she had already gone through.

But then something caught her eye. She looked closer at the red rose. There she found what looked like a spot on the shirt. It blended in with the rose, which caused her to miss it at first. But it was definitely a spot on the shirt. She wasn't certain, but it looked like blood. She looked closer at the rest of the rose and found one smaller spot.

Dani carried the shirt carefully to the bed, leaving the shirt on the bed, she then returned to the hamper. She next pulled out a pair of light gray sweat pants. She examined them closely and found nothing of interest. She added the pants to the pile on the floor and continued looking at the last few items in the hamper.

The chief asked Dotty how often she would go to Stacy's house.

Dotty answered, "Oh, all the time. We were best friends. That's why your intrusion here is so ridiculous."

Dani finished with the last few items in the hamper, and found nothing with blood stains. For the time being, she left the dirty clothes on the floor. She wanted to get photos of the hamper and of the items that were in it before she returned the small pile of dirty clothes to the hamper. She went out to her squad car to get a crime scene investigation kit and while returning to the bedroom, she nodded at Eric to join her in the bedroom. Eric entered and Dani pointed to the shirt on the bed.

Eric looked at the shirt and shrugged, then said, "I don't think it's going to fit you."

"Take a real close look at the rose," Dani stated.

Already wearing his latex gloves, Eric carefully picked up the shirt and looked at the rose. Seeing what appeared to be a spot, he looked closer, and then muttered, "Bingo."

Dani asked him to photograph the shirt, which he did. Then, while she carefully placed it in a clear evidence bag, Eric photographed the closet, the hamper and the pile of clothes on the floor. Dani then returned the other clothes on the floor into the hamper and then continued her search.

Eric returned to the kitchen and continued to look for anything that might be used as a murder weapon.

Dani examined all of the items on the shelves in the closet and then started with the shoes. She examined all of the tennis shoes and any other shoes that looked like they would be worn while doing yard work. She found an old pair of sneakers with red shoe laces that had grass and dirt stains on them. She examined both shoes very carefully and found one small spot of what looked like blood. It was located at the exact spot where the fabric and the rubber sole come together. She put the shoe in an evidence bag and placed it on the bed next to the bag with the shirt in it.

She continued her search in the closet and then went through the drawers in the two dressers in the bedroom. She did not find any socks, gloves, hats, nor any other clothing with blood stains. Nor did she find anything which could have made the wound in Stacy's chest.

The chief asked Dotty if she used the gate in the back fence to get to Stacy's or if she walked around the block when she went to visit Stacy.

Dotty answered, "Well, I used the gate, of course. That's why we had it put in. We both used it. We just have to be sure to keep the hedge from covering it up. I have to trim the hedge along the gate all the time."

The chief thought about what Dotty had just said. Then he excused himself from Dotty and asked her to stay on the couch. He went into the kitchen to speak with Aaron who was working with Eric. He told Aaron to go into the garage and search in there, looking for any type of hedge clippers.

Dani came out of the bedroom and nodded to the chief, indicating that she had found something. She then went to the laundry room to check the washer and dryer. Neither had any clothes in them. Dani then began to look for any notepad, letters, or any correspondence that might give evidence of an ongoing argument between the two. Meanwhile, Eric had completed his search in the kitchen. He had found a couple of steak knives and a few other sharp knives, but none appeared to be wide enough nor thick enough to match the description of the wound. He did find a clever, but again it didn't seem to match what they were looking for. Dani asked him to return to the bedroom to get a photo of the shoe which was in the evidence bag. Eric did so, and then joined Aaron in the garage.

The chief asked Dotty when the last time was that she had used the gate between her house and Stacy's.

Dotty thought for a minute. And then thought some more. Finally she answered, "Last Sunday afternoon. We had a glass of tea on the patio while Kortnee and Kolton played in the yard. It was a very peaceful moment." Dotty then began to cry.

Aaron and Eric found a row of gardening tools along the far wall of the garage. Hanging from some nails in the wall, they found a rake, a shovel, a hoe and a push broom. Next to them was a workbench cluttered with a variety of hand tools, a bag of potting soil, a few empty flower pots, and a watering can. Below the bench were a couple of drawers. The top drawer contained a few simple tools: screw drivers, pliers, a small hammer, a pair of wire cutters. The next drawer also contained some tools: a few adjustable wrenches, a socket set, two larger screw drivers, a small level, a drill.

Still wearing the latex gloves that he had put on in the kitchen, Aaron opened the third drawer and froze for a moment. He said, "Hey, Eric, take a look at this." There, next to a spray nozzle for a garden house, a small digging tool, and a pair of brand new gardening gloves, lay a pair of hedge clippers. The clippers were the kind that could be held in one hand. The clippers were closed. Together the two blades were about two and a half inches wide, about five inches long.

Eric said, "Let me get a few photos before you bag it."

The chief gave Dotty a minute or two to compose herself.

He then said, "I know that you have a very hectic schedule, like most of us. Is there any chance that you've been over to Stacy's since Sunday, and just simply forgot?"

Dotty looked away for a moment and then said, in what seemed somewhat defiant to the chief, "No. I have not been over there since Sunday."

Eric took photos of the clippers. He then photographed the workbench, from a couple of angels and different distances. He then took photos of the entire garage, being sure to show the location of the bench. Aaron then placed the clippers in an evidence bag.

Aaron then closely examined the work gloves. They looked as if they had never been used. A sales tag was still stapled on the wrist of one of the gloves.

Aaron looked at Eric and said, "I wonder where the old gloves are?"

Eric replied, "I'm guessing they'll never be found." He was right.

Eric returned to the kitchen and motioned for Dani to join him there. Aaron continued to search the garage. He did not find any other gloves, work shoes, hats or rags that might contain evidence. He did a quick look in the trash cans but found nothing of interest there. He then joined Dani and Eric in the kitchen. She let them know that she did not find any notes between Dotty and Stacy. Then Dani went into the living room and nodded for the chief to go into the kitchen. Dani remained with Dotty.

Dani asked Dotty, "Have you and Stacy had any arguments lately?"

Dotty, indignantly replied, "Oh, here you go again with your gossip magazine type questions."

Dani replied calmly, "Please, just answer the question."

Dotty glared at Dani and said, "No. We don't fight. We are best friends. We were like sisters."

Dani said, "Well, sometimes sisters argue. Sometimes best friends argue. But they get over it. Are you saying that you and Stacy never argued?"

Dotty looked a little confused for a moment, but then said stubbornly, "No. That's why we've been best friends for so long. We just get along, very naturally."

At that moment Chief Earl reentered the room. Dani stood up and the chief slowly sat down. Eric and Aaron came in carrying the evidence bags and placed them on the coffee table.

The chief picked up the bag containing the t-shirt and said, "Dotty, is this your shirt?"

Through the clear bag she could see the red rose on the front of the shirt. She nodded and said, "Yes. That's my shirt. Why do you have my shirt in a bag and why are you going through my dirty laundry? What's going on!?"

The chief ignored her question and then held up the bag with the shoe and said, "Does this look like one of your shoes?"

"Yes," Dotty said abruptly.

The chief then asked, "And are these your gardening clippers?" as he held up the bag containing the clippers. Dotty silently stared at the clippers. She glanced at the chief and then looked back at the clippers. The chief waited, but Dotty said nothing.

The chief then said, "Dotty, we found these in your garage, are they your clippers?"

Dotty again looked at the chief, then back at the clippers, she then whispered. "Yes. They look like mine."

The chief then said, "Dotty, there are blood stains on the shirt and on the shoe. We'll turn the clippers over to the lab to examine, but I'm guessing there is blood on them as well. Can you tell me how that blood got on these items? Also, can you tell me who's blood it is that is on them?"

Dotty sat, stunned, silent. She stared at the items, but did not answer.

"Dotty?" the chief said. But still, Dotty did not say a word.

Then a tear trickled down her cheek. Just one at first, but soon followed by more. Then she cried. The police officers waited patiently, sadly. Dotty sobbed and sobbed. The chief nodded to Eric and then to the evidence bags. Eric took the bags out to his squad car.

When she had stopped crying, the chief said, "Dotty Miller, I am placing you under arrest for the murder of Stacy Pruitt. Please stand and put your hands behind your back while Dani puts you in handcuffs. I want you to listen very carefully while Aaron reads you your rights."

Dotty didn't move, Dani reached out to take her arm, but Dotty jerked away. Dani looked at the chief and as he stepped around, Dani stepped back. The chief gently took her arm, she looked up at him and then slowly stood. Dani carefully placed the handcuffs on her wrists. Dotty stared at the chief the entire time, not saying a word.

Aaron said, "Dotty Miller, You have the right to remain silent.
Anything you say can and will be used against you in a court of law.

You have the right to an attorney.

If you cannot afford an attorney, one will be provided for you.

Do you understand the rights I have just read to you?"

Still, Dotty said nothing. The chief asked, "Dotty, do you understand your rights?"

She nodded her head slowly and said softly, "yes."

Then she looked at the sheriff and through her tears she whispered, "I didn't mean to do it. Stacy was my best friend. I didn't mean to kill her."

Aaron and Dani just stared. It was, perhaps, one of the saddest moments either had experienced as a police officer.

The chief, still looking at Dotty, said softly, "It's probably best that you don't say anything more until you talk to an attorney. Do you have an attorney, Dotty?"

She shook her head no.

The chief continued, "One can be provided for you or perhaps you would like to hire one. Your parents might be willing to help with that. Would you like for me to call your parents?"

She looked up at the chief and slowly nodded yes. Again she began to cry.

The chief said, "I'm going to have you ride with me back to the station. I'll call your parents from there."

Chief Earl told Aaron and Eric to see if there were any computers or electronic communication devices. If so, they were to bring them in to be examined by the County Attorney's office. They were then to secure the house, including the do not cross, yellow police tape across both front and back doors.

He then took Dotty Miller to the station and placed her in a cell.

Chapter Seventeen: Murder In A Small Town

Early the morning of Stacy's murder, Dotty had retrieved a pair of pruning shears and her gardening gloves from her garage and went into her back yard to do some gardening. She loved the early hour of the morning. She dressed comfortably for this task. She was wearing a white t-shirt, gray sweat pants and a comfortable pair of old tennis shoes with red shoe laces. The t-shirt had a single red rose on the front. It was her favorite gardening shirt. She put on a light jacket, but as she began to trim her flowers, she took the jacket off and laid it across a chair on the back patio. She enjoyed the cool briskness of the morning. She looked forward to the mornings when she would spend a little time in her back yard, trimming and gardening. She found it to be peaceful, relaxing, one might even say, therapeutic. But this morning took a turn for the worse.

As she worked her way into the far corner of the yard, she began to trim the hedge by the gate between her yard and Stacy's. That's when Dotty saw her, sitting there on her back porch, all beautiful, even at this early hour of the morning. Sitting by the house that she got in her divorce from Shane. Sipping her coffee and reading one of those glamour magazines. Not a care in the world. As if she were a queen sitting on her throne.

Dotty moved away from the gate and continued to trim some of her flowers. But there was now more intensity in her trimming. She aggressively hacked away at her plants. The more she thought about her friend, the angrier she became.

Friend? Ha! That was a one way street. She had been a loyal and faithful friend to Stacy. But what had Stacy ever done for her? Nothing! She was all take and no give. Everything always revolved around Stacy. What kind of a friend would steal your boyfriend: not once, but twice! It was bad enough to have that happen in high school, but now, again, as adults. How could a true friend do such a thing? True friend? What a joke. Best friend? What a cruel, terrible, awful joke. Self-absorbed, heartless, backstabbing friend.

She worked her way back to the gate and Stacy still sat there. Without a care in the world. Little Miss Prissy.

Dotty opened the gate, still carrying her pruning shears, and entered Stacy's yard. Stacy saw her and smiled. She said, "Well, aren't you the industrious one. Up early and doing your gardening. You go girl!"

Dotty said nothing, as she slowly walked toward Stacy.

Stacy said, "The kids spent the night at mom and dad's. They were going to take them to school this morning. There's coffee in the kitchen. Help yourself."

Dotty thought to herself, "Help yourself. Help yourself. Can't even get up and get a cup of coffee for your best friend. If I were one of your many boyfriends, you'd be all over that cup of coffee, but hey, it's just me. Best friend. Loyal to a fault. Faithful friend. Help yourself. Back-stabbing friend. Back-stabbing traitor. Back-stabbing neighbor. Back-stabbing….back-stabbing…stabbing…"

And then, Dotty snapped.

She had reached the porch and stood next to Stacy, staring.

Stacy looked at Dotty's expression and said, "Dotty, what's wrong. You look like you're going to explode. Are you alright?"

Dotty said nothing. Stacy continued, "Dotty?"

And then, Stacy stood up.

For reasons she could not understand, for reasons she could never explain, for reasons that made absolutely no sense whatsoever, Dotty raised her pruning shears into the air, and before Stacy could comprehend what was about to happen, using both hands, Dotty suddenly plunged the shears into Stacy's chest. One anger fueled, pent up burst of adrenaline, powerful stab. Just one. But that's all it took.

Dotty pulled the shears back and held them in front of herself. Stacy immediately fell to her knees, gasping. She looked up at Dotty and softly mumbled, "Dotty?" and then fell forward. Dotty lowered the shears and immediately looked around. She did not see nor hear anyone or anything.

Blood was dripping from the shears, falling into the pool of blood which was quickly expanding around Stacy. Dotty put her hand under the shears to catch any additional drops, and took a step back before the expanding pool of blood reached her old white tennis shoes with the red shoe laces. She looked around again, looked down at Stacy one last time and then slowly walked back to her yard.

She closed and latched the gate and went immediately into her kitchen. There, she took off her gloves and carefully washed the shears. Then she returned the shears to the workbench drawer. She returned to the kitchen and saw the blood stained gloves still sitting next to the sink. She placed the gloves into a brown lunch bag and placed the bag on the workbench in the garage. She went back to the kitchen and meticulously scrubbed her kitchen sink and the surrounding countertop, making certain that there weren't any traces of blood.

Afterward, she went into her bedroom, then into her closet where she undressed, dropping her clothes on the floor, and then went in to take a shower. While in the shower she began to cry, and then to sob uncontrollably. Eventually she got out of the shower, dried off, put on her robe, and crawled into bed. She was trembling, but she didn't move from her bed for over an hour.

Once she decided to get out of bed, she dressed and went into the kitchen to make herself some coffee. "Help yourself," echoed in her mind. Her hands started to shake, so she put the coffee down and walked over to the kitchen window and looked toward her back fence. The large hedge along the fence kept her from seeing into Stacy's backyard or the porch. The only view was through the gate, which was near the end of the fence line. She thought about walking out to the gate, but began shaking again and decided against it.

She went into the living room and turned on the news. She stared at the TV but had no idea what was being said. She cried again. She had no idea how long she had been sitting on the couch before she finally got up and went back into the kitchen. She tried again to get a cup of coffee. This time she was successful and sat at her kitchen table, slowly sipping the coffee while eating a breakfast protein bar.

She then went back into the bedroom to put on some makeup and to do her hair. Laying on the closet floor were the clothes she had been wearing when she went into the yard to do her gardening. She quickly looked the clothes over for any traces of blood. Seeing none, she dropped the clothes into the nearly empty hamper. She placed her old sneakers back into the closet.

She decided that she couldn't just sit in the house all day, so she made up her mind to go to the market. She went into the garage and as she went around to the driver's side of the car, she noticed the brown lunch bag which contained her gardening gloves, still sitting on the workbench. She picked up the bag and then got into her car and drove over to the gas station. She dropped the bag containing the gloves into the trash can, and then topped off her gas tank. She then drove over to Truman's Market to pick up a few things.

As she slowly drove to Truman's, she noticed that the street was soaking wet but didn't remember that it had rained. Weird, she thought. She pulled into the parking lot and parked her car. Before she reached the door, one of her friends, Amie, asked if she had heard the terrible news about Stacy.

Dotty smiled and said, "No. What's she up to now?"

Amie blurted out, "She's dead! They found her laying on her back porch. The news is spreading all over town."

Dotty just stared at Amie, expressionless.

"Dotty, are you okay?" Amie asked.

Then Dotty said, "You must be mistaken. It's just a terrible rumor. Stacy can't be dead. No way."

Amie cautiously explained, "No Dotty. It's true. I'm sorry. I know she was a good friend of yours. But it's true."

Dotty said, "Good friend? I was her best friend." Then she started to cry. Amie gave her a hug as several people passed by, looking, but then awkwardly hurrying along.

After a few moments Amie offered to give her a ride, "Do you want me to take you anywhere? Do you want me to take you home?"

Dotty quickly replied, "No. I've got to go to Stacy's house. I've got to be there for her."

She then turned and hurried to her car. She drove over to Stacy's and pulled up in front of Officers Eric and Dani.

Chapter 18: Epilogue

When they arrived at the station, Dotty was placed into a cell while Aaron began to fill out the paperwork for booking. Chief Earl called the County Attorney, Mark Prescott, to inform him that they had made an arrest in the Stacy Pruitt murder. When informed that the suspect was Dotty Miller, there was a pause on the other end of the line.

The chief asked, "Surprised?"

Mark replied, "Well, I guess there's not much that surprises me anymore. But this comes pretty close!"

The chief said, "Yep. I hear ya."

"What evidence are you giving me to work with," Mark asked.

The chief explained, "Well, for starters, she made a confession. Three of us heard the confession."

"And you had read her, her rights?" Mark questioned.

"Absolutely," the sheriff said. "Additionally, we'll give you the murder weapon, found in Dotty's garage, which matches the victim's wound. It appears to have been washed clean. I assume you'll have your guys tear it apart to look for any remnants of blood. We'll also give you a shirt and a shoe, both Dotty's, with blood spots on them. I'm confident DNA analysis will match that with the victim."

Mark said, "Great. I'll be over in an hour or so, and you can fill me in on all of the details."

"Will do," the chief responded. "We'll turn the evidence over to you at that time, as well."

"Good job, Chief," Mark commented.

"Thanks, Mark. The ball is in your court now, so to speak," the chief said.

"Court is what I do," Mark quipped. "We'll continue to communicate through the entire process. See you soon."

Dotty's parents hired an attorney for her case. The blood stains on Dotty's t-shirt and shoe were all a match with Stacy's DNA. The gardening shears had a small amount of blood between the blades where they are connected by a screw, in spite of Dotty having washed off the rest of the blood. It was a small amount, but enough to run a DNA test. It, too, matched Stacy's DNA.

With that evidence in hand, a search warrant for Dotty's office at the salon was issued. Her office computer was confiscated and the contents examined. The one-way airline ticket and hotel reservations for Rio de Janeiro were discovered and included in the list of evidences in the case against Dotty.

Once the defense attorney examined all of the evidence, and was told that Dotty had made a confession, he began the usual positioning to get the best plea bargain he could get for her.

Ten months after the arrest, Michelle walked into Chief Earl's office and said, "I have County Attorney Mark Prescott on line one."

"Thanks, Michelle," the chief said as he picked up his phone and hit the button for line one.

"Good morning Mark, how's your case load been lately?" the chief began.

Attorney Prescott said, "Well Chief, the pile keeps getting higher and higher. There's a lot of bad guys doing a lot of bad things out there."

"Sad but true, Mark, sad but true," the chief replied. He then added, "What can I do for you this morning?"

"Just wanted to update you on the Dotty Miller case. The judge agreed to the plea bargain we struck with the defense. She pleads guilty to a reduced charge of manslaughter, instead of second degree murder. She'll get sixteen years, out in fourteen with good behavior," Mark explained.

The chief thought for a moment and asked, "They didn't press for temporary insanity or some such thing and then psychiatric treatment?"

"And then some shrink let's her out in four or five years? Don't even get me started on that issue!" Mark declared.

"I hear ya," the chief agreed. "You've got a heck of a tough job to do. We appreciate all that you're doing over there. Keep up the good work."

"Thanks, Chief. You, too," Mark said. "Talk to you soon."

After hanging up the phone, Police Chief Frederick Earl leaned back in his chair and thought about the friends he had made over the years in Springerville: Fire Chief Gary Patrick, Judge Hardman, Barb Huff, Chaplain Bill Bergeson and many others. Life in small town Springerville was good. The chief couldn't help but smile.

By this time the chief and his officers had settled back into their routine of law enforcement. Springerville had returned to once again being a quaint, peaceful small town in middle America. Unfortunately, they would quickly learn that the Stacy Pruitt murder would not be the last murder to rock this small town ...

Made in the USA
San Bernardino, CA
29 January 2018